Prai

"Balaban unleashes hilarious McGrowl. . . . Filled with absurd humor and fun, cartoonlike action."
— *USA Today,* review of
McGrowl #1: *Beware of Dog*

"Mr. Balaban takes his obvious love of language and wordplay and creates a magical tale of a mind-reading dog that all young minds should read. An intelligent and plentiful debut."
— *Jamie Lee Curtis*

"For anybody who has ever had a dog, loved a dog, or wanted a dog. A great adventure beautifully written. I hope Bob writes the next one about me."
— *Richard Dreyfuss*

Read all the books about

#6

PUPPY
TALES

Bob Balaban

A Storyopolis Book

STORYOPOLIS™

AN
APPLE
PAPERBACK

SCHOLASTIC INC.
New York Toronto London Auckland Sydney
Mexico City New Delhi Hong Kong Buenos Aires

With thanks to a loyal reader
Bethany Jackson
for good advice and kind thoughts

ISBN 0-439-43459-9

12 11 10 9 8 7 6 5 4 3 2   5 6 7 8 9 10/0
                                              40

Printed in the U.S.A.
First Scholastic printing, March 2005

Contents

CHAPTER ONE
Christmas Presence

Thomas Wiggins flew down the corridor and headed straight for his locker. The bell for last period was still ringing in his ears. It was the start of winter break. The rest of the middle school followed close on Thomas's heels, trumpeting like a herd of joyful elephants.

"Listen up, listen up!" Principal Grimble shouted over the loudspeaker. "I have an important last-minute assignment for each and every one of you." He paused dramatically, and everyone immediately stopped talking. "Have a really great vacation! And that's an order!" A rousing cheer of relief went up from the students. And everyone was off and running again.

"Merry Christmas, Alfred," Mabel Rabkin, Stevenson Middle School's ancient and much-loved registrar, called cheerfully to Thomas from her office on the far side of the hall.

"Thanks," Thomas replied without missing a beat. Mrs. Rabkin had recently celebrated her ninety-second birthday. Although she was thoroughly devoted to each of her "trusty seedlings," as she referred to the students, remembering their names was not always possible. Or even likely.

"Come on over, Stephen," Mrs. Rabkin added. "Don't be shy."

Thomas quickly turned on his heels and ducked into Mrs. Rabkin's office. She was sitting at her desk, wearing the same raggedy Mrs. Claus outfit she insisted on dragging out every holiday season. An enormous red hat trimmed with fake ermine came down so far over her ears that the rest of her nearly disappeared.

"Ho, ho, ho!" she exclaimed. Her eyes twinkled and she smiled merrily. She picked up some sleigh bells from her desk and jingled them at Thomas.

"Almost forgot," Thomas said as he dug into his book bag and pulled out a small, neatly wrapped present and deposited it on her desk. Thomas's mother always made sure to buy holiday gifts for all of the Stevenson faculty.

"You're a good boy, Norman. Don't let anybody tell you that you're not," Mrs. Rabkin said. She reached into the pocket of her Mrs. Claus costume and proudly handed Thomas a moldy candy cane. It was covered with lint and red fuzz and appeared to be at least as old as she was.

"Gee, thanks, Mrs. Rabkin," Thomas said,

quickly shoving the striped treat deep into his own pocket. "Looks delicious."

"Don't eat it all at once, Freddy," she warned. "You might get a stomachache."

Stomachache? Thomas thought. *I would probably drop dead right there on the spot.*

Mrs. Rabkin went back to sewing glittery muslin wings onto a bunch of angel costumes for today's Christmas assembly. Thomas didn't have the heart to tell her that the assembly had taken place several hours earlier.

Thomas sped down the hall to his locker, threw on his coat and scarf, and ran outside into the icy air. His breath formed billowy clouds, and his cheeks stung from the chill the moment he was out the door. Winter had arrived in full force.

He ran over to greet his dog, McGrowl, who had been patiently sitting on the front steps for the last half hour, waiting for his boy to get out of school. The golden retriever leaped up and licked Thomas all over his face. Thomas patted his side with one hand and ruffled the hair that stuck up on the top of his head with the other.

McGrowl poked his big brown nose into Thomas's pocket and rummaged around desperately for the candy he knew was hiding there. "Down, boy," Thomas commanded sternly.

McGrowl sent a telepathic message hurtling back. *Fat chance!* he replied. Thomas chuckled as he received the message. The dog could look into Thomas's mind and understand exactly what he was thinking as easily as he could look into Thomas's pocket and see that there was a special Christmas treat waiting for him.

Just then McGrowl emerged triumphant, grasping the moldy candy cane firmly between his lips. In less than a second he had scraped off the excess fuzz with his teeth and swallowed the minty confection. Thomas hoped his dog's stomach was as indestructible as the rest of him.

"Last one to Ralph's house is a rotten egg!" Violet Schnayerson called as she sped past. Violet happened to be Thomas's best friend. She also happened to be an excellent sprinter.

"Wait for me," Thomas cried as he raced to catch up. Lewis Musser, the class bully, elbowed his way forward and joined in the chase, as did Sophie Morris, who, though small for her age, was still one of the faster runners in the class.

The entire sixth grade was invited to a skating party at Ralph Sidell's house. Ralph's dad, Elmer, had dug a small pond in their backyard. The last few days had been bitterly cold, and the ice on the pond was finally thick enough to skate on safely. Ralph was suddenly the most popular boy in Stevenson Middle School. At least until the ice melted.

PUPPY TALES

As McGrowl raced along, he kept tripping over his paws. McGrowl wasn't usually clumsy, but today he was wearing the dreaded protective rubber booties Thomas's mother always made him put on at the first sign of winter. "Remember," she had warned him earlier that day, "salt on an icy sidewalk in the evening can be very harmful to an unprotected paw in the morning." Mrs. Wiggins had an opinion to offer on just about every subject.

McGrowl had first come to live with the Wiggins family a brief two years ago. Thomas's mother had protested his arrival vehemently. Now, Mrs. Wiggins had come to love McGrowl almost as much as Thomas did. She not only enjoyed his company, she always spoke to McGrowl as if he could understand every single word she was saying. Which did, in fact, happen to be true.

McGrowl was a bionic dog. If he wanted to, he could leap tall buildings in a single bound.

Or use his X-ray vision to look inside the buildings if he didn't happen to feel like leaping over them. McGrowl could, of course, communicate with Thomas telepathically, and his power of smell was astonishing. A little salt under one of his pads was hardly likely to cause the dog even the slightest inconvenience.

Thomas and Violet had taken great pains to guard McGrowl's amazing secret. Just as Superman protected his identity under the guise of the mild-mannered Clark Kent, McGrowl avoided detection by pretending to be an ordinary golden retriever. Only he didn't wear glasses.

There were two other individuals who knew the truth about McGrowl. The evil Milton Smudge and his wily assistant, Gretchen Bunting, had entered the picture quite by accident. Having learned about McGrowl's bionic abilities, the two villains concocted a terrible plan. They would enslave the dog and use his powers to help them take over Thomas's hometown, Cedar Springs — and then the world. Several times they had nearly succeeded. But each time, Thomas and Violet had helped McGrowl successfully avert their attempts.

Only last spring, in fact, Thomas had managed to hypnotize Smudge and Bunting, erasing their memories. Then he'd sent the two villains hurtling through space in a small but powerful rocket ship. The ship deposited them on a desert island so remote it didn't even have a name. The possibility of their return was slight, but enough to keep Thomas and McGrowl ever on the alert.

The entire sixth grade sprinted down Chestnut Street, laughing and shouting and heading straight for the fork in the road that led to Mulberry Lane and Ralph Sidell's house. "Only three more blocks to go," Thomas cried, in the lead. Lewis Musser was in second place and not too happy about it. Violet was running a close third. McGrowl brought up the rear. Even with his booties, he had to take care not to run *too* quickly. Everyone in Thomas's grade knew and loved McGrowl, but no one suspected he had bionic powers.

When a light snow started falling, everyone began to sing a spontaneous chorus of "Jingle Bells." McGrowl couldn't resist joining in. He howled along, carrying the entire bass harmony part all by himself.

The group arrived, panting and huffing, at Ralph's backyard. Lenny Winkleman, the class hypochondriac, had clearly won the rotten egg award. He had gotten snow in his eyes and lost precious minutes waiting for his vision to clear. Ralph's dog, Willie, an enormous Irish wolfhound, ran out to greet everyone. He barked and jumped around, catching snowflakes in his mouth and making a general nuisance of himself.

PUPPY TALES

Everyone strapped on ice skates and crowded onto Ralph's pond. They skated and pushed and fell and laughed and had the time of their lives. Toes were numb from the cold, and noses were red and running.

Lenny, having recovered fully from "snow in the eye," strained his wrist while throwing a snowball and spent most of the evening watching the proceedings from the Sidells' living room window. He wrapped his arm in the compression bandage he carried with him at all times and managed to complete his entire holiday reading assignment before the night was over.

Miss Thompson, Thomas's English teacher, had volunteered to help the Sidells chaperone the party. She brought out big mugs of hot cider for everyone, even McGrowl. "In honor of this glorious evening," she announced proudly, "I shall recite a poem I learned in the fifth grade." Everyone skated off the pond and gathered around to listen. Miss Thompson said:

"Snow, snow, snow.
White, white, white.
I can see it, even with my bad eyesight."

After the applause died down, she gave a lesson in skating backward and engaged in a brief but lively game of ice hockey with some of the better players.

After most of the activities died down, an exhausted Thomas and Violet and McGrowl headed for home at last. They were wet and cold and tired but filled to the brim with hot cider and holiday cheer.

As Violet started up the path to her front door, McGrowl sent Thomas a telepathic message.

Please, he begged. *May I go in and say hello to Miss Pooch?*

Without giving it a second thought Thomas sent back a resounding *yes*, and the three friends wiped their feet and paws on the Schnayersons' doormat, brushed the snow from their coats, and waited to be let inside.

"You kids hang up your stuff," Violet's mom said as she scurried back into the kitchen. "I'm up to my elbows in dough." The delicious aroma of cinnamon and brown sugar filled the room.

"Are they almost ready, Mom?" Violet asked expectantly. Mrs. Schnayerson was not generally known for her cooking abilities. The list of things she did well was long but didn't, for the most part, include kitchen skills. She did, however, bake an uncannily appealing Christmas cookie.

"Anybody seen Miss Pooch?" Violet's older sister, Alicia, asked as she ran downstairs and started looking under tables and chairs. "She was here a minute ago."

"She couldn't have gotten very far," Thomas said as everyone joined in the search. McGrowl's powerful nose and trusty X-ray vision had already determined that the missing dog was in the garage. He quickly let Thomas in on the secret.

"Think she's in the garage?" Thomas asked innocently.

"It's worth a try," Alicia replied. And they all went to the garage to look for the errant pet.

CHAPTER TWO
Parenthood

Miss Pooch was McGrowl's constant canine companion. The little bulldog-Chihuahua mix belonged officially to Alicia. But the entire Schnayerson family claimed ownership of the bullwawa, as they affectionately referred to her.

The dog was famous for her bad behavior and unpleasant temperament. But in the last few months she had undergone an enormous change. She had been stubborn and unyielding. Now she was easygoing and responsive. She had been disobedient and willful. Now she was cooperative and even good-natured. Thomas was certain this change in her behavior was the result of one amazing fact: Miss Pooch was going to have puppies. And McGrowl was the proud father.

McGrowl was not only excited about becoming a dad, he was also relieved by the change in Miss Pooch. Not that he hadn't been crazy about the "old" Miss Pooch. It was just that the "new" bullwawa was a lot . . . easier.

McGrowl enjoyed the little dog's company tremendously. He never tired of looking at her spiky fur and undershot jaw. He found her perky ears a wonder and her squinty little mismatched eyes adorable. Together, they spent many happy hours chasing the neighborhood cat. Miss Pooch could run and jump and wrestle as well as any dog McGrowl had ever known. She was filled with fun and mischief. But up until now, she'd hardly seemed an ideal candidate for motherhood.

As the three children and the dog tiptoed into the garage, Alicia put her fingers to her lips. "Shhh," she warned. "Don't startle her."

At that very moment, Miss Pooch was putting the finishing touches on what Alicia called the nursery. This was a cozy area in a corner of the garage specially selected for the puppies to sleep in once they arrived. A large flannel-covered pillow sat on the floor near the water heater. Mr. Schnayerson had cleaned out all the old newspapers and magazines that had previously occupied the space. Miss Pooch was picking up with her teeth some tools Mr. Schnayerson had left on the floor, and was carefully depositing them far from the nursery.

"Looks like her mothering instinct has really kicked in," Violet whispered.

"Yeah," Thomas answered quietly. "Big-time."

Mrs. Schnayerson had put up cheerful curtains in the garage windows, and Violet helped out by laying down some indoor-outdoor carpeting for the puppies to play on. McGrowl's offspring would be warm and comfortable here. They would be happy. They would be safe. And if McGrowl had his way, the evil duo would never, ever know of their existence.

"Look, guys, she's arranging her pillow," Violet whispered as she watched Miss Pooch carefully push around the large, soft square with her paws and nose. McGrowl immediately went to help her. Together they pushed and pulled at the pillow. When it was just the right degree of fluffiness and perfectly situated, Miss Pooch lay down, exhausted, in the middle of her handiwork. McGrowl rested one of his large paws gently over her shoulders and nuzzled her belly with his big brown nose. He growled contentedly.

McGrowl couldn't wait for the puppies to be born. He would play with them. He would teach them to catch a ball and chase a Frisbee. He would show them how to behave properly. He would take care of them. *But when would they arrive?* He shot Thomas an anxiously telepathic message. *When?*

"Soon, McGrowl, soon," Thomas whispered. Dr. Minderbinder, the vet, had said it would be at least another week before the puppies would be born. McGrowl was so excited he could hardly stand it. Thomas couldn't wait, either. He was more than a little curious to see what bull-wawa–golden retriever puppies would look like.

"Let's go, boy," Thomas said quietly. He hated to disturb his friend, but Mrs. Wiggins would soon be worrying where they were. With Christmas so close at hand, Thomas wasn't taking any chances in the naughty-or-nice department. McGrowl licked Miss Pooch a fond good-bye on the top of her head and quickly trotted off to join Thomas. Miss Pooch put her head down and fell promptly asleep.

Violet said, "Bye, McGrowl. Bye, Thomas." Then she asked Thomas, "Want to come over tomorrow and work on our science project?" Gosling Fletch, their esteemed science teacher, had given out his annual holiday assignment. Students had been directed to "make an improvement to an existing invention." The best project would win a prize. Thomas and Violet had already begun work on their new and improved lie detector.

"Good idea," Thomas said as he put on his scarf and helped McGrowl on with his booties. "Though I need to squeeze in Christmas shopping somewhere. "A certain dog I know sent me a Christmas list a mile long."

"Guess I know which one that was," Violet joked, scratching McGrowl behind his ear.

Thomas wasn't kidding. McGrowl had created an enormous wish list. Hamburgers and a new collar were only a few of the many items he had requested. Along with a new Frisbee, hot dogs, several books on parenting, potato chips, and a can of tennis balls. Instead of mailing the list to Santa, the dog simply sent it telepathically to his boy.

As he trotted home alongside Thomas, McGrowl looked around carefully for evidence of Milton Smudge and Gretchen Bunting. Thomas immediately sensed the dog's apprehension and sent him a telepathic message not to worry. *They're gone for good this time, pal. I promise.*

McGrowl looked up at him. Thomas could see from the expression on the dog's face that he still wasn't one hundred percent certain. Thomas had to admit that he wasn't, either.

But it was winter break. And more snow was predicted. Christmas morning was coming soon. And so were Mrs. Wiggins's famous holiday strudels. And so were McGrowl's puppies. Four cuddly, noisy, adorable little balls of fur.

Thomas stuck out his tongue and thought about how much he loved winter vacation. He caught as many of the swirling flakes as he could and decided that maybe, just this once, it wouldn't be such a bad idea to send his worries about the evil duo on a vacation as well.

CHAPTER THREE
Doctor's Orders

It snowed all night long. In the morning, Thomas awoke to find the front lawn covered with a frosty white blanket, knee-deep and just waiting to be played in and molded into snowmen and icy forts. Thomas rolled over in bed and listened to the muffled sounds of his father's shovel as it scraped out a path from the garage to the street.

McGrowl turned over on his belly and sent Thomas a telepathic request. *Rub, please.* Thomas leaned over and rubbed. *Harder, please.* As Thomas scratched and rubbed,

McGrowl growled contentedly, and Thomas thought about his good fortune. Fourteen days of no school. Two whole weeks of McGrowl every day, and puppies to look forward to.

It didn't take a bionic nose to smell the delicious scent of pancakes and bacon drifting up from the kitchen. McGrowl sat up, shook himself awake, and pleaded with Thomas to get out of bed. "Five more minutes," Thomas said, as he stretched lazily.

The dog refused to take no for an answer. He jumped up on the bed and pushed at Thomas with his big furry head until the boy tumbled onto the floor. "Have a heart," Thomas pleaded.

McGrowl just shook his head and sent Thomas another telepathic message. *Feed me!* So Thomas put on his robe and slippers, combed his hair, and hurried down the stairs.

* * *

"More bacon please, Dad," Thomas asked. He and his older brother, Roger, were seated at the kitchen table, napkins on their laps, plates laden with mounds of food. McGrowl sat at their feet, licking the edges of his empty bowl. The dog had finished his chicken-flavored kibble nuggets and gravy in a single gulp.

He had also finished every bit of pancake and bacon the boys had managed to sneak him. *More anything, please,* McGrowl begged Thomas in his most appealing telepathic voice.

You'll get sick, Thomas responded swiftly.

Mr. Wiggins flipped the next batch of pancakes in a series of brisk maneuvers before approaching the table carrying an enormous platter of crisp, perfectly done bacon. It smelled so good McGrowl considered grabbing the entire batch out of Mr. Wiggins's hands with his mighty mouth.

Thomas issued an emphatic telepathic *Don't you dare!*

McGrowl wrestled with his inner food demon and managed to restrain himself. It was a good thing he did so. Mr. Wiggins was terrified of McGrowl.

Thomas's father knew his fear wasn't rational. He knew there wasn't a kinder, gentler dog than McGrowl. Unfortunately, self-help books and tapes had done little to remedy the situation. Try as he might, Mr. Wiggins never felt entirely comfortable in the dog's presence.

"Bxffhhshandcbhslkdtheruupleese," Roger mumbled. His mouth was so full of bacon no one could understand what he was saying. Even McGrowl was unable to decipher a single word.

"Say again, please, Roger?" Mrs. Wiggins asked politely. She was seated at her desk in the corner by the window, with her calculator and a stack of papers. "Try swallowing first," she added. "This isn't a barnyard, honey."

"Nobody told him," Thomas said. He grinned at his brother and made a loud *oinking* sound. Roger was famous for his terrible table manners.

"May I have some napkins, please?" Roger said, swallowing. He glared at Thomas as he kicked him under the table.

Without waiting for a new napkin, Roger wiped his mouth on his pajama sleeve, picked up his syrupy plate in his hands, and licked it clean. Then he burped loudly, got up from the table, and went over to the refrigerator to pour himself another glass of milk.

"Honey, have you ever heard of utensils?" Mrs. Wiggins asked. "Honestly." She shook her head and continued adding and subtracting an enormous column of numbers. "Two thousand six hundred and twelve," Mrs.

Wiggins announced proudly. "What do you think of that?"

"Honey, that's wonderful," Mr. Wiggins exclaimed, wiping his hands on an oven mitt. "I'm so proud of you."

McGrowl looked up from his bowl, bacon and pancakes clinging to his muzzle, and sent out a telepathic *me, too*.

"Me, too, Mom," Thomas piped up. "Only what I am I being proud of?"

"Your mother has sold a record number of Momsicles this month, kids," Mr. Wiggins explained. Even Roger was impressed. He didn't say anything about it, though. His mouth was too full.

"You kids better finish up your breakfast," Mrs. Wiggins said as she put on her apron and rubber work gloves. "In five minutes, I start today's production."

Every day after Thomas and Roger left for school and Mr. Wiggins went to work, Mrs.

Wiggins made batch after batch of her recent invention, Momsicles. With McGrowl's help (though Mrs. Wiggins didn't ever realize McGrowl had helped her) she had created a foolproof recipe for a delicious and healthy between-meal snack. A cross between a Popsicle, a cake, and a pudding, they contained more vitamins and minerals than a hungry man's dinner.

The success of Momsicles far surpassed Mrs. Wiggins's greatest expectations. What had started as a whim had turned into a whirlwind. Mrs. Wiggins had somehow tapped into an enormous unfilled niche in the snack food marketplace. A niche that seemed to know no bounds. Everyone loved her Momsicles. And even better, everyone bought them. They were literally flying off the shelves.

Mr. Wiggins had created a simple but effective advertising campaign. There wasn't a person within fifty miles who hadn't heard his catchy slogan, "Momsicles are great to eat, put one in every lunch box," sung to the tune of "Yankee Doodle Dandy." Mr. Wiggins had also designed the cheerful and eye-catching Momsicle container. It was both attractive and useful. Made entirely from recycled cardboard, when empty it could be used as a pencil holder, a change purse, or a carrying case for insects.

A small plastic magnifying glass was included with every purchase. The bug part had been McGrowl's idea. He had suggested it to Thomas, who had, in turn, suggested it to his father. The dog was extremely proud of his useful contribution.

Mrs. Wiggins put away her paperwork and took out a stack of bowls and spoons. "Make sure you're all back in time to help with dinner," she said. "We're having company." Thomas and Roger put their plates in the sink and ran upstairs to get ready for the day.

McGrowl licked the floor under the table and quickly followed them.

"Company" usually was code for Mr. Wiggins's boss, Al Lundquist, and his wife, Dot. "Don't go to any trouble on our account," Mr. Lundquist had said when Mr. Wiggins invited him to dinner several days earlier. "We love leftovers." Al Lundquist knew that in Mrs. Wiggins's case leftovers were likely to be filet mignon with mushroom ragout topped off by a side of cherries jubilee. Al Lundquist loved dinner at the Wigginses' and looked for any excuse to come over.

Of course, there would be no leftovers served at tonight's feast. Mr. Wiggins helped prepare the kitchen for the morning's assembly line before rushing out to begin a furious round of shopping. First a quick trip to the butcher, then the organic vegetable market, then finally the French bakery on the far side of town for just the right meringue shells.

*   *   *

Meanwhile, Alicia and Miss Pooch were at the vet's with Mr. and Mrs. Schnayerson. Violet was at home waiting for Thomas so they could work on their lie detector.

Now that the puppies were almost due, barely a day went by without a visit to kindly Doc Minderbinder and his loyal nurse, Leona Trask. The doctor looked into Miss Pooch's mouth and examined her pointy little ears. Then he listened to Miss Pooch's stomach with his stethoscope to make sure the hearts of all four puppies were beating strongly.

"Is everything okay?" Alicia asked nervously.

"Couldn't be better," the doctor said, smiling. "Puppies and mother are all doing beautifully. Congratulations, Miss Pooch!" Doc Minderbinder placed the bullwawa on the special doggie scale. She didn't even wriggle. "Hmm," Doc Minderbinder mumbled.

"We seem to have put on a few more ounces."

"Go easy on the snacks, folks," Nurse Leona wisely observed. "We're careful to watch for obesity in our pregnant females."

"I had no idea it was such a problem," Mrs. Schnayerson observed.

"Honey, it's more than a problem," Nurse Leona proclaimed. "And don't get me started on iron deficiency."

"Gosh," Mr. Schnayerson said. "You sure know a lot about animals."

"That's why they pay me the big bucks," Nurse Leona joked. And then she sashayed into the other room, only to return in a few moments with a tray of freshly laundered towels and cloths.

"She *has* been eating more than usual, Doctor," Mrs. Schnayerson whispered, her voice tinged with concern.

"Nurse Leona's always been on the heavy side," the doctor said under his breath as he continued to examine his canine patient. "I see no reason to worry."

"I meant Miss Pooch, Doctor," Mrs. Schnayerson explained. Indeed, just the other evening the bullwawa had sneaked into the living room, climbed onto the coffee table, and consumed an entire platter of smoked salmon in less than a minute. "Is that normal?"

"It wouldn't be normal if she *wasn't*," he replied. "She's eating for five now! Just watch desserts and carbohydrates."

Doc Minderbinder carefully examined Miss Pooch's eyes and nose. The little dog was unusually cooperative. She turned her spiky little head this way and that so the doctor could observe her more easily.

The kindly vet wasn't even surprised. He had seen many an unruly dog turn into an obedient and mature parent. But sometimes, it was the other way around. Lanny Wilson's dog, Muggles, who had won first prize in every state obedience trial in her division, became so unruly during her pregnancy that poor Mrs. Wilson had to move into a hotel until the puppies were born. After that, Muggles immediately reverted to her former, well-behaved self.

"As you know, the average dog pregnancy lasts between fifty-nine and sixty-one days," the doctor said as he rapped gently on Miss Pooch's chest. "Good, good," he muttered.

"They could be born any minute," Alicia said, panic rising in her voice. "Shouldn't we go home right away?"

"She probably has a few days left," Nurse Leona said crisply. "Of course, this isn't an exact science."

"Four little Miss Pooches, honey, just think," Mrs. Schnayerson said as she smiled at her husband.

"I'm thinking," Mr. Schnayerson said as he stared back at Mrs. Schnayerson with a look that seemed to combine both the warm glow of anticipation and absolute terror.

"Gosh, Miss Pooch," Alicia warned as she got out her collar and leash. "You're going to have to take extra-good care of yourself." Miss Pooch wagged her crooked tail happily.

As they put on hats and mittens and scarves, Dr. Minderbinder handed Mrs. Schnayerson a list of instructions. "Don't worry. She'll do just fine," he said in a calm and reassuring voice.

The Schnayersons walked the ten blocks home. By now the sidewalks were cleared, but mounds of newly fallen snow were heaped to one side. Miss Pooch was having the time of her life. She was receiving enormous amounts of attention. She was being fed three times a day instead of the usual old boring once in the morning and once before going to bed. As far as she was concerned, things couldn't have been better.

A huge snowdrift caught her eye. The bull-wawa trotted over to the edge of the sidewalk and dived headlong into it. She wriggled about joyously. "Careful, Miss Pooch," Alicia called nervously.

Miss Pooch loved everything about winter. Especially snow. She couldn't wait to introduce it to her puppies. They would play in it when they were a little older. But not without coats and scarves and protective rubber booties. McGrowl would see to that.

Just then Officer Nelson came strolling by and tipped his policeman's hat. "Merry almost Christmas to all you happy people," he said, twirling his nightstick around cheerfully.

He had pinned a little plastic Santa Claus right under his badge. Its nose lighted up when its long white beard was pulled, and a small computer chip buried inside called out a "happy holidays" greeting in a high-pitched mechanical voice. "How's my favorite bull-wawa?"

"She's due any day now, Officer," Violet's mother replied. The friendly policeman reached into his pocket and took out a tiny chocolate Christmas tree. He held the candy out to Miss Pooch.

"Oh, she would never eat that. She's very strict about her pregnancy diet," Alicia said proudly. Indeed, Miss Pooch didn't appear to be the slightest bit interested in it.

She was, however, absolutely fascinated by Officer Nelson's Santa pin. As the man stood up she suddenly grabbed the pin in her razor-like teeth and refused to let go. "Get her off of me!" Officer Nelson cried, in a sudden panic.

The pin's nose glowed a bright red as Santa repeated his happy holidays greeting over and over. And over. Alicia finally managed to pull Miss Pooch away, leaving Santa recognizable, although somewhat disfigured.

Officer Nelson backed away slowly. "Keep that dog away from me. She's not normal!" he said as he hurried away. Impending motherhood had definitely improved Miss Pooch's behavior, but it hadn't changed everything. As Alicia was fond of saying, "Once a bullwawa, always a bullwawa."

"Naughty, Miss Pooch," Alicia scolded. "Very, very naughty." But then Alicia relented, as usual, picked up the little dog, and kissed her on the top of her head. She could never stay angry at the bullwawa for more than a few seconds. "You didn't mean to be bad, you're just overtired," she cooed. "We'll take you home right away."

And with that, the Schnayersons made their way home without further incident.

CHAPTER FOUR
Who's That Knocking?

Back at the Wigginses', Thomas and his father were helping Mrs. Wiggins do the dishes. Thomas's mom had finished her Saturday batch of Momsicles and left a sinkful of dirty pots and pans and Momsicle molds in her wake.

McGrowl was busy drying. Using his tail as a wind machine, he quickly blew off the water from the surface of an assortment of gleaming silver utensils. His peculiar drying technique never left unsightly streaks.

Suddenly, a knock on the door sent Mrs.

Wiggins running out to investigate. "Who could that be?" she asked Mr. Wiggins. "Are you expecting anyone, honey?"

"Maybe Santa got the date mixed up and he's coming early," Mr. Wiggins joked.

"But Dad, Santa always comes in through the chimney," Thomas reminded him.

"Silly me," Mr. Wiggins replied.

McGrowl loved hearing about the jolly fat man with the white beard and the red coat. He wasn't exactly sure where the North Pole was, but he knew it wasn't anywhere in the vicinity of Cedar Springs. McGrowl didn't find it the least bit surprising to learn that Santa traveled in a sleigh pulled by eight flying reindeer. After all, McGrowl himself had some pretty unusual skills.

Are you sure Santa's really coming? McGrowl asked Thomas telepathically. The dog had gotten into some serious trouble last week when he chased Olivia, the cat, into a phone booth and nearly knocked it over in his excitement. McGrowl wasn't exactly certain of the precise definition of *naughty,* but he was pretty sure Santa wouldn't think chasing a cat, no matter how annoying, was nice.

Don't worry, pal, I'm sure saving the world from evil is gonna qualify you for a lot of great stuff, Thomas beamed back. McGrowl was so relieved he jumped up and licked Thomas on the face, frightening Mr. Wiggins so badly he dived into the broom closet where he pretended to be searching for a dustpan.

Meanwhile, Mrs. Wiggins peeked through the curtains and discovered none other than her long-lost cousin, Milton Gompers, staring back at her. "Oh, my," was all she could say. She hadn't seen Mealy Miltie, as he had been known, since he was sixteen years old and she was a girl of twelve. And now there he was, standing on her front porch, his hat in his hand and his parrot, Burlington Birdy, on his shoulder.

"Let me in, *awk*," the parrot squawked loudly. "*Awk*, let me in." Mrs. Wiggins immediately experienced two conflicting impulses. On the one hand she felt like bolting the door, running upstairs, and hiding under the bed. On the other she felt like rushing out and throwing her arms around her relative.

He was, after all, the last and only remaining member of a particularly remote branch of the family. Miltie and his parents, Sally and Montrose Gompers, had moved down south after experiencing some difficulties with the law regarding a number of possibly unfounded charges of insurance fraud and perjury while under oath. The family had vehemently denied the entire affair.

Nonetheless, a scandal had erupted that rocked the community and sent the Gompers packing so quickly they were unable to leave a forwarding address. The only information Mrs. Wiggins had ever gathered about her wayfaring relatives was that the Gompers clan had settled somewhere in Georgia and had left behind a trail of unpaid bills and forged checks in their wake.

Just as Mrs. Wiggins had decided on bolting, running, and hiding, Roger came rushing down the stairs. He was on his way to his bowling league playoffs. He flung open the front door before his mom had a chance to stop him and ran past his long-lost relative. Mrs. Wiggins was left staring uncomfortably at Miltie, who threw his ample arms around her, all the while exclaiming, "Mah deah long-lost relation! What a joy and pleashuh to see y'all!" in a booming southern accent. It was impossible not to notice the enormous steamer trunk standing on the porch behind him. Evidently, Miltie was planning on staying for quite some time.

McGrowl watched the proceedings from behind a sofa in the living room. He had left the dishes to dry on their own for a moment and crept in silently to observe the new arrival. His ears sat back on his head, a certain sign that the dog was suspicious of something. The appearance of any stranger, especially one with the name of Milton, put McGrowl on high alert.

This Gompers fellow was large and perfectly friendly-looking. He had a bushy head of thick black hair parted neatly in the center and wore round horn-rimmed glasses. In fact, everything about the man was round. He had round fleshy hands and a bulbous round nose. Even his mouth seemed to form a near-perfect circle as he exclaimed "Oh, mah! Oh, mah!" over and over.

Surely, McGrowl thought, *even the ingenious Milton Smudge wouldn't be so cunning as to use his own real first name to throw us off guard.* The dog sniffed the air. Not a trace of formaldehyde anywhere. Although he had managed to successfully disguise it in the past, the foul-smelling odor tended to cling to Milton Smudge like a monkey to a banana.

Upon taking a second, deeper sniff, McGrowl detected the powerful aroma of gardenias. *Either he's trying to cover up his telltale acrid scent,* McGrowl mused, *or he likes cheap cologne.*

By now, Thomas had tiptoed quietly out to the living room, where he joined McGrowl behind the sofa. *Think that's Smudge?* Thomas asked.

McGrowl shrugged. *Maybe. But where's Bunting?*

Gretchen Bunting was capable of many ingenious disguises. *Could she possibly have disguised herself as a parrot?* Thomas wondered. It seemed way too far-fetched.

I doubt it, McGrowl responded. *But it's not out of the question.*

Mrs. Wiggins was so taken aback by the arrival of her cousin she could barely speak. The parrot took one look around the house and flew immediately to the top of a bookcase in the living room. She looked down and loudly screeched, "Get lost, *awk.* Get lost." Mrs. Wiggins looked up at Burlington. The bird made a threatening gesture with its beak and squawked, "Bad girl. Bad girl!" The bird's vocabulary seemed to consist entirely of unpleasant expressions. McGrowl took an instant dislike to both the parrot and her unctuous owner.

"That theyah's Burlington Birdy," Miltie explained. "She's mah parrot, as y'all can see. She's friendly but awful protective, so watch out, becuz . . ."

"I bite, I bite!" the bird shrieked, finishing Miltie's sentence and flapping her wings.

"Mah parrot and ah would be much oblahged if we could stay with y'all fo' the Christmas holidays," Miltie added.

Mrs. Wiggins stared at her new arrivals. Her mouth opened and closed wordlessly.

"Perhaps y'all didn't heah me. Ah was sayin' . . ."

"I'll just go tell my husband you've arrived," Mrs. Wiggins finally said, mustering up as much welcoming good cheer as she was able. "He won't believe his ears." And, indeed, he didn't.

CHAPTER FIVE
To Tell the Truth

Miltie Gompers spent the rest of the day at the Wigginses' house regaling Mr. and Mrs. Wiggins with stories of the Gomperses' checkered family history. Thomas and McGrowl went to Violet's house and labored over their lie detector in the Schnayerson basement, Thomas's favorite place to spend a Saturday morning.

"Could you hand me the pliers?" Violet asked. "And tell me more about this round guy."

"Sure," Thomas answered. "Got any more copper wire?"

"All gone. How about tungsten?" Violet asked. She tossed a spool of the silvery thread over to Thomas.

"There's not much to tell," Thomas began. "He's either my mother's long-lost cousin or he's Milton Smudge in disguise. Either way, he's staying for Christmas."

"What's that parrot all about?" Violet asked.

"Either the world's meanest bird or Gretchen Bunting in disguise," Thomas said as he wrapped rubber coating around the wire.

"You're telling me Bunting can fly now?" Violet asked dubiously. "I don't think so."

"She can do a lot of other stuff," Thomas said.

"Yeah, well, maybe the bird's some kind of decoy. You know, to throw us off the case. That kind of thing," Violet said idly as she twisted some thin metal tubing together with the pliers. "The bird's last name begins with a

B. Maybe that's a clue, too. I don't know. Got a screwdriver?"

The new and improved lie detector was coming along nicely. It was due the day after vacation but was almost all done.

Thomas had learned a lot about lie detectors in *Popular Inventors Digest.* He had received a subscription for his birthday last year and read every issue from cover to cover. He had been especially interested to learn that passing a lie detector test was not, in and of itself, proof positive that the truth was being told. Under the right combination of circumstances, a lie might not be detected, or a truth might register as a falsehood.

"There's gotta be a way to make a better one," Thomas had said to Violet the day Mr. Fletch handed out the assignment. "One that doesn't make mistakes."

Violet had been in complete agreement. "Let's give it a try," she concurred. And so over the past several weeks the two of them had accumulated all of the equipment they imagined might help them do just that: transistors, rubber tubing, and just about every kind of gear and gizmo imaginable. All these materials were piled in front of them on Mr. Schnayerson's already overcrowded workbench.

"I'll be happy if we only achieve, say, ninety percent accuracy," Thomas said to Violet, as he carefully examined a series of interlocking flywheels.

"But it might be nice to win a prize," Violet said as she selected some flexible zinc tubing and attempted to snake it in and out of some holes in a square of predrilled Masonite. "Last year Ralph Sidell won with his low-salt version of cheddar cheese, remember?"

"True," Thomas replied as he handed the pliers to McGrowl, who trotted over to Violet, carrying them in the soft folds of his mouth.

"And Mr. Fletch gave honorable mention to Sophie Morris for her chemical analysis of dog food," Thomas added, smiling. "I mean, anybody could analyze dog food."

But not anybody could eat it, McGrowl thought. He had sampled just about every popular brand of the food reserved for his kind. No matter how many dogs he saw on television eagerly scarfing down bowls of the stuff, he still couldn't figure out what was so great about it. As far as McGrowl was concerned there was nothing in the world that could compare with anything that came out of Mrs. Wiggins's oven. He would do just about anything for a bite of one of her cream-filled butterscotch brownies.

Suddenly, they all heard Miss Pooch scratching frantically at the basement door. McGrowl ran over to let her in. Using his mouth and his paws, he was able to turn the knob and open the door.

"What's up with Miss Pooch?" Thomas asked. The bullwawa definitely seemed more agitated than usual.

She hurtled into the room, running this way and that and sniffing about excitedly. Before McGrowl had a chance to even think about stopping her, she selected just the right spot in the corner of the room and squatted.

"I thought she was supposed to be house-broken," Thomas ventured.

"Me, too," Violet replied.

Me, three, McGrowl thought.

And then, just as quickly as she had entered the room, Miss Pooch ran back upstairs again and into the kitchen. She didn't stop whining until Alicia had fixed her a snack and poured her a fresh bowl of water.

McGrowl grabbed some paper towels in his mouth and brought them over to Violet, who quickly wiped up Miss Pooch's accident. McGrowl sent Thomas a telepathic message:

Forgive her. She's not herself. Thomas smiled. McGrowl raced upstairs to make sure the mother of his puppies didn't make any more "mistakes."

"Something's up," Thomas said as he reached for the superglue.

"Think it's — you know — time?" Violet asked softly.

"It's not supposed to be," Thomas answered as he attached the base of the lie detector to the rest of the machine. "But she sure is acting strangely."

Meanwhile McGrowl arrived in the kitchen just in time to watch Miss Pooch gobble up her second helping of scrambled eggs and liver snaps. The bullwawa was ravenous. As soon as she was done she went over to her place by the stove, curled up, and went to sleep. So McGrowl returned to the basement.

For a moment the three friends sat lost in thought in front of their creation. Then Violet poked the appropriate wires into appropriately tiny holes, Thomas finished attaching the base to the top, and McGrowl carefully plugged the cord into the outlet with his teeth.

The three young scientists stepped back to admire their handiwork. Even McGrowl was impressed. The lie detector was a formidable-looking invention, indeed, from the bottom of its gunmetal base to the top of its gleaming glass-and-plastic removable cover.

"Think it really works?" Violet asked.

"Only one way to find out," Thomas replied, and started hooking himself up to a number of color-coded wires that led to the machine.

"Let me help with that," Violet said as she attached one of the wires to Thomas's wrists. She made sure the connections were tight on the blood pressure cuff that encircled his forearm, while McGrowl checked out the suction cups that secured the wires that measured the pulse rate on Thomas's temples.

Smaller wires were attached to each of his fingertips. They measured the degree of moisture and the temperature of Thomas's skin. If a person lied, his or her skin frequently reacted with a slight rise in body temperature and an increase in sweating, known as the GSR, or galvanic skin response. Thomas was eternally fascinated by these details.

"You look like Frankenstein," Violet chuckled, once Thomas was connected to the device.

"Ask me," Thomas replied.

"Ask you what?" Violet answered back.

"Ask me if I'm Frankenstein," Thomas said as he leaned over and flipped the switch on the machine. It made a loud whirring sound as it started up. The needles on the dials that covered the side of the machine immediately started jumping around.

"Okay," Violet said. "Are you Frankenstein?"

You better not be, McGrowl thought.

Thomas smiled as he replied, "Yes, I am."

What? McGrowl thought. *Say it isn't so.*

As Thomas spoke, a loud buzzing sound emanated from the machine, and the dials swung around wildly.

"The machine says you're lying," Violet said happily, reading the printout as it emerged from the side of the machine. McGrowl gave a big sigh of relief.

"It works!" Thomas exclaimed. "Ask me something else."

Violet thought for a moment before she asked, "How old are you?"

"I am eleven years old," Thomas responded quickly.

The machine buzzed and hummed and spit out a piece of paper before grinding to a halt. All humming and whirring ceased as Violet picked up the printout and read it aloud. "You are definitely lying."

The friends looked at each other and sighed. Evidently, they still had a little work to do on their project. And then Thomas noticed that McGrowl had sat on the cord and pulled it from the wall by mistake.

"Mind plugging that back in, fella?" McGrowl looked around sheepishly, took the plug in his teeth, and plugged it right back in. The machine began to hum and whir all over again and spit out another piece of paper. Thomas proudly read the different, correct response. "The truth, the whole truth, and nothing but the truth."

"Eureka!" Violet shouted. "It works. It really works."

Thomas and McGrowl looked on proudly. The machine did, in fact, appear to be an accurate predictor of the truth.

CHAPTER SIX
Food for Thought

"Say hello to the Lundquists, Thomas," Mr. Wiggins said, wiping his hands on a dish towel. Al and Dotty Lundquist had arrived a good half an hour early, and Mrs. Wiggins was still in the kitchen putting together the hors d'oeuvres while everyone gathered in the living room.

"Hello," Thomas responded obediently. He and McGrowl had just returned from the Schnayersons'. They had barely enough time to wash up, throw on a fresh shirt, (or, in McGrowl's case, a fresh collar), and run downstairs to greet their important visitors. Roger was having dinner at a friend's house.

"My, isn't he getting big," Mrs. Lundquist gushed while smiling at Thomas. For reasons unknown to Thomas, this always seemed to be the first thing guests said to him. Surely he hadn't grown all that much since his previous encounter with Mrs. Lundquist at the supermarket last Tuesday.

"You stink, *awk*! You stink," Burlington suddenly shouted, and swooped straight down from her living room perch at Mrs. Lundquist's face, wings outstretched. The bird squawked loudly, and changed directions abruptly, missing Mrs. Lundquist by inches.

"What an interesting pet," Mrs. Lundquist said as she eyed Burlington nervously. "Is she friendly?"

"She's a regulah jokah," Miltie apologized. "She jus' luhves people. And children. And dawgs. Doncha, Burlington?"

"Ha!" Burlington laughed from the mantel-piece as Miltie Gompers laid a pudgy hand on Thomas's shoulder. "Ah'm so happy weah gawna get to know each othah at last," he said. "Ah will be stayin' heah for the duration of the holidays, thanks to the kahndness of y'all's daddy."

McGrowl regarded Thomas's long-lost relative with the funny accent and feathered friend suspiciously. Then Mrs. Wiggins glided into the room with a tray of her famous pupu tidbits, a variety of Polynesian bite-size delights. Ever the gracious hostess, she placed them carefully on the coffee table and raced back into the kitchen to start the broccoli.

Mrs. Lundquist immediately grabbed one and popped it into her mouth. "Interesting texture," she said as she bit down hard on a piece of sweet-and-sour chicken. "Ahh!" she screamed. "My tooth!"

In her haste, Mrs. Wiggins had failed to fully defrost one of the hors d'oeuvres, and Mrs. Lundquist had chipped a molar. As she ran to the bathroom to check out the damage, Mrs. Lundquist slipped on the rug and fell to the floor, yelling out in pain.

Mrs. Wiggins came running to see what was the matter. "Don't worry about me, I'm perfectly fine," Mrs. Lundquist explained weakly, clutching her arm to her side. "I'll just freshen up for a moment. Be right back." And then she proceeded to lock herself in the bathroom for a good fifteen minutes. Thomas and McGrowl exchanged worried glances. This did not bode well for the dinner ahead.

After a certain amount of pleading and cajoling on the part of Mr. Lundquist, Mrs. Lundquist returned to the living room, and everyone went to the dining room and sat down. There everything went smoothly. For a while. At least no more teeth were chipped, and Burlington remained blissfully quiet. She was preoccupied with the tasty meal of seeds and nuts Mrs. Wiggins had thoughtfully prepared for her.

"Those are absolutely delicious. What do you call them again?" Mr. Lundquist asked when dessert was served.

"Momsicles," Mr. Wiggins replied as he passed around a platter of the delicious snacks.

"Stacey invented them, Albert," Mrs. Lundquist interjected somewhat harshly. "I've been meaning to pick up a pack. They're sold in every store imaginable. Everybody's talking about them. What rock have you been living under?" She grabbed one for herself and immediately began devouring it. She could hardly have been hungry. Despite her toothache, she had consumed nearly as much beef Stroganoff and broccoli à la Wiggins as her portly husband had.

What she was, was irritated. And when she was irritated she ate.

"Oh, I see. Well, well," Mr. Lundquist mumbled, and continued eating. "That's good to know."

"Ah do declayah," Milton Gompers began in an awkward attempt to get the conversation back on track. "These thangs are bettah than sweet potato pie," he said, taking a bite of his Momsicle. "Wheyah evah did y'all get the recipe?" he inquired innocently.

"She invented them, you idiot!" Mrs. Lundquist snapped. Thomas glanced up, wondering if Miltie knew about McGrowl's role in inventing Momsicles. Was he really Milton Smudge? Burlington, who had finished her meal by now, suddenly flew at Mrs. Lundquist again, this time landing right on top of her head. The bird clung to her hair with her powerful claws, reached over, and started pecking feverishly at the woman's eyebrows. Fortunately, Mrs. Lundquist had long, thick bangs that prevented the bird from doing any serious damage. Mr. Wiggins glanced around nervously, horrified at the impression his family was making on his boss.

Mrs. Lundquist could restrain herself no longer. "Get that thing away from me!" she hollered at the top of her lungs. "It's a menace to society." And then she jumped up from her place at the table, spilling her glass of wine, a rare 1987 Bordeaux. She flung her napkin at the bird as hard as she could. Burlington caught the napkin in her beak, tore it into shreds, and scattered the pieces onto Mrs. Lundquist's head.

"I hate Christmas," the parrot taunted. "I hate Christmas! *Awk!*" And then, while Mrs. Lundquist cowered in the corner, Burlington Birdy tore the last remaining shred of Momsicle out of Mrs. Lundquist's hands with her powerful talons and popped it into her mouth.

"She's just showin' her affecshun. She loves y'all," Miltie explained feebly. It was clear who ruled the roost in this relationship.

"She sure has a funny way of showing it," Mr. Lundquist said, and chuckled. Much to his wife's dismay (and Mr. Wiggins's relief), he seemed to find the entire incident hilarious.

After several unsuccessful attempts Miltie was at last able to corner Burlington and remove her to her cage in the den, where the distraught bird shrieked so hysterically she rendered normal conversation impossible.

The dinner guests fell silent, except for the occasional shouting of a "PASS THE SALT, PLEASE!" McGrowl put his paws over his ears and, for the first time in his life, found himself wishing Olivia were around. Olivia loved birds. Especially for dinner. Fortunately, Burlington soon exhausted herself and fell into a deep sleep. Mr. Wiggins was still on edge. It would soon be time for Christmas bonuses. Tonight's disastrous meal was not likely to have filled his boss with the spirit of holiday giving.

Thomas took two Momsicles, unwrapped them both, and passed one down to McGrowl who was sitting under the table secretly studying Miltie's shoes. Thomas sent the dog a telepathic message. *Notice anything strange?*

Are you kidding? McGrowl replied. *Everything about this guy is strange.* Careful inspection of the shoes, however, had revealed nothing more unusual than a clump of mud and weeds and a bit of used chewing gum stuck to Miltie's heel.

"Attention, everyone. May I have your attention, please," Mr. Lundquist asked, as he rapped his spoon loudly against his coffee cup. Mr. Wiggins clenched his teeth and prepared himself for the worst.

"Let us lift our glasses high," Al Lundquist began. "Or in this case shall we say our coffee cups." He laughed loudly at his own joke. Everyone else was too worn out to even pretend to be amused. He continued.

"A toast to a wonderful dinner. A terrific bunch of friends. And most especially to the amazing talents of a very special fellow we call Henry Wiggins."

Thomas couldn't believe his ears. Mrs. Wiggins's jaw dropped. Mr. Wiggins nearly fell off his chair. He had been expecting to be fired. Or demoted. Or chastised at the very least. Mr. Lundquist paused as he waited for the applause to start. There wasn't any. Everyone was too stunned to react. Even Miltie had nothing to say.

Unfazed, Mr. Lundquist went on. "I have

some amazing news. I have decided that you, and you alone, Henry Wiggins, have been selected to head my new office in Wauwatosa, Wisconsin. Add one big notch to that impressive belt of yours. And call it Senior Regional Vice President in Charge of Promotion. What do you think about that?"

His joyous proclamation was met with resounding silence. Thomas stared down at his plate numbly. Would they have to move to *Wisconsin*? Was this the end of his wonderful life in Cedar Springs? Would he be leaving Stevenson for good? How would he tell Violet? He couldn't even pronounce the name of the stupid city, anyway. It sounded like a terrible place.

Mrs. Wiggins wasn't exactly overjoyed about the turn of events herself. She, unfortunately, knew all about Wauwatosa. Her nephew Seymour Fish had moved there years ago, never to be heard from again. It was very small.

And very cold. And very, very far away, indeed. She wasn't entirely sure they had mail delivery there.

McGrowl had his own set of concerns about moving. He was about to become a father. He could hardly leave Miss Pooch behind to care for a brood of lively little puppies all on her own. He was far too responsible for that. And besides, he didn't want to miss a single day of their puppyhood. It was absolutely out of the question.

"So what do you have to say for yourself, Mr. S.R.V.P. — and I think you know what those initials stand for." Mr. Lundquist chuckled, as he downed another cup of coffee.

Mr. Wiggins just shook his head as a million thoughts raced though his mind. He couldn't just uproot his entire family and transplant them to a city they had never even visited. He wasn't even exactly sure how to spell it.

On the other hand, this was a once-in-alifetime proposition. He would make more money than he'd ever dreamed. Mr. Wiggins had wanted a career in advertising on the national level for as long as he could remember.

Henry Wiggins was a born salesman. In the second grade, he had painted stars and rocket ships on clothespins and made close to a hundred dollars selling them as conversation pieces to his schoolmates.

"Over fifty uses," he had proclaimed. "And that's not including the one for which they were originally intended." He wrote that slogan when he was seven years old, and his mother still had it hanging over her mantelpiece.

But how, he thought, *can I possibly accept this position? And yet how can I not?*

Thomas stared at his father, not daring to breathe, waiting for his fate to be determined. Would he really have to move away and leave his life here behind? McGrowl looked on anxiously, too. Would his puppies be raised without the benefit of a father's love? Would he ever see Miss Pooch again?

"We're waiting," Mr. Lundquist said. "Speech, speech!"

Mr. Wiggins cleared his throat before he began. He opened his mouth. Nothing came out. He cleared his throat again.

"Get to the point already, will you, Wiggins?" Mr. Lundquist barked sternly. "We haven't got all night."

Mr. Wiggins looked at Thomas. His son tried not to think about how sad he was and how much he would miss his friends. His teachers. The house he had grown up in. He knew every nook and cranny of it by heart. He thought about how he would miss Miss Pooch and the puppies. Disappointment was etched indelibly all over his face.

And then Mr. Wiggins took a long, hard look at Mrs. Wiggins. She was doing her best to appear supportive and encouraging but she looked absolutely miserable, as well. She loved her life in Cedar Springs. She loved her Momsicle business. She loved her neighbors. She knew just about everybody in the little town. And the ones she didn't know she was looking forward to getting to know. She loved her kitchen. She loved her garden. A tear glistened in her eye. Miltie looked at his long-lost relative sympathetically.

"Time marches on, Henry!" Mr. Lundquist shouted peevishly. He was not a man who enjoyed being kept waiting.

"I guess what I mean to say is" — Mr. Wiggins bit his lip, took a deep breath, and started again — "What I mean is, umm . . ." Thomas's stomach did flip-flops as he waited for his father to speak.

"It's a great thing you are doing for me," Mr. Wiggins said at last. "I am thrilled. I am excited."

Mr. Lundquist smiled broadly.

"And . . . I have absolutely no idea what I am going to do," Mr. Wiggins concluded.

When the Lundquists decided to leave several minutes later, Mr. Wiggins was still wringing his hands and staring silently down at the table.

"Guess he's still thinking it over," Mr. Lundquist said as he put on his overcoat and boots. "Funny, I thought he'd be pleased."

"Oh, I think he is," Mrs. Wiggins explained. "Terribly pleased." She paused awkwardly. "I just think it's an awful lot of good news for a person to absorb all at once."

"Honey, do you think you could get me out of this place before that terrifying bird attacks again?" Mrs. Lundquist urged. Luckily, Burlington was still sleeping.

And then the honored guests were gone, tromping off into the blustery cold evening. Dishes were washed and floors were mopped. Leftovers were put into plastic containers.

Miltie and Burlington went up to the guest room. And all the while everybody did his or her best to avoid talking about the ominous decision that was staring them in the face. The veritable elephant in the room.

Roger came home, and Thomas relayed the bad news to him. Depressed, Roger immediately went to bed.

Thomas almost felt as bad for his father as he did for himself. Mr. Wiggins sat in the dining room staring into space for a long time. Then he sat in the den staring into space. And finally, he sat in his bedroom and stared into space.

As exhausted as everybody was, nobody fell asleep quickly that night. "We'll get through this, pal, you'll see," Thomas said to McGrowl, who happened to also be staring into space.

CHAPTER
SEVEN
Wee Paws

Just as the Wiggenses were falling asleep, Alicia was waking up. "Down, Miss Pooch, down," she said groggily, and pulled her pillow up over her ears. Miss Pooch had been scratching at the side of Alicia's bed for what seemed like hours.

This, in itself, was not unusual. When Miss Pooch needed to play, she needed to play. And when Miss Pooch needed to be taken out, she needed to be taken out. Lately, she'd been getting cravings and simply could not be appeased until a craving was met. Last week it had been ice cream. The week before, sardines. Alicia sat up and rubbed the sleep from her eyes.

"Wait a minute," Alicia said, yawning, as she threw on her robe and slippers. She assumed Miss Pooch needed to go for a walk. "I'll get your leash. Hold your horses." But Miss Pooch continued whining and scratching. There was something decidedly different about the bull-wawa's behavior. Something in the tone of her whine. Even the expression on her funny little face. Miss Pooch was trying to tell her something, Alicia realized.

And then it dawned on her. "Oh, my gosh," she said. "You don't want to go out, do you? It's happening, isn't it . . . you're — you're . . . MOM!" Alicia shouted, as awake now as if someone had hurled cold water in her face. "Come quick! IT'S HAPPENING! HURRY!" she screamed, kneeling down to attend to her dog.

In seconds, Mr. and Mrs. Schnayerson were racing down the hallway. "We're coming," Mrs. Schnayerson screamed hysterically. "Stay calm!" Violet came careening out of her bedroom to see what was happening and nearly knocked them both over.

"Everybody remain calm!" Mrs. Schnayerson yelled again. "There is absolutely no reason to panic." And then she tripped over her slippers and nearly fell down.

"Is there a fire or something?" Violet asked.

Just then, Alicia arrived in the hallway carrying Miss Pooch. She spoke quietly and firmly and with enormous confidence.

"She wants me to take her to the nursery in the garage. It's time," Alicia said. And with that, she and Miss Pooch walked swiftly but calmly down the stairs and off to the garage. Violet couldn't help but wonder whether her sister and Miss Pooch shared the same telepathic connection as Thomas and McGrowl.

*   *   *

"Are you sure?" Thomas asked a few seconds later. He sat up in bed and held the receiver tightly to his ear. Violet had called to tell him the exciting news. McGrowl woke up immediately and dashed over to the phone.

"Come quick," Violet said. "She's having her puppies. It's really happening." McGrowl jumped up and down with excitement. And then he was off and running down the hallway.

"But she's not due for a few more days at least," Thomas murmured groggily.

"Well, nobody told Miss Pooch," Violet replied. "You better get over here right away. Gotta run. Don't want to miss anything." And then, with a *click,* she was gone.

"What's going on?" Roger asked, waking up. Thomas explained quickly, climbing out of bed.

McGrowl appeared in Thomas's doorway, panting eagerly, holding an assortment of hats and scarves and gloves in his mouth. He didn't want to miss a thing, either. Roger, Thomas, and McGrowl threw on their coats and raced down the stairs. Mrs. Wiggins and an exhausted Mr. Wiggins got out of bed and learned the exciting news.

"Wait for us," Mrs. Wiggins called to her sons and McGrowl. "We'll be down in a jiffy." And then she turned to her husband and tried to hurry him along with a quick "Don't dawdle, honey, we're gonna miss the whole thing." Mr. Wiggins could hardly tell his excited wife that was precisely his plan. He was about as eager to watch four puppies being born as he was to go to the dentist and have a cavity drilled, but he followed reluctantly. As she flew down the hallway Mrs. Wiggins decided to leave Miltie and Burlington asleep in the guest room. Mrs. Wiggins wasn't sure how the irascible bird would react to something as small and defenseless as puppies.

At the Schnayersons', Alicia sat on the garage floor and did her best to make the bullwawa feel comfortable. "It's all right, Miss Pooch. Breathe deeply," she said reassuringly. "You're gonna be all right."

"She still seems kind of worried to me," Violet said, looking on.

"Of course she's worried," Alicia replied softly. "She doesn't know what's happening. Dr. Minderbinder says we all have to be very supportive. Tell her how you feel about her," she said to her sister.

"I don't know," Violet demurred.

"Go on," Alicia urged.

"I'm not much of a dog talker, really," Violet said, blushing.

"You can do it," Alicia prodded. "Miss Pooch needs you."

"All right," Violet said as she searched for just the right words. "You're about to have puppies, Miss Pooch," she said at last, stroking the bullwawa's head gently. "And I bet they're going to be really cute. And incredibly healthy. And I think you'll be a really good mother. And I really like you a lot and . . . that's all, I guess. Bye for now." Violet felt incredibly self-conscious. She knew that, unlike McGrowl, Miss Pooch couldn't really understand what she was saying.

"She definitely liked that. She's much calmer. Look," Alicia said. It did indeed appear as if Miss Pooch had appreciated Violet's kind sentiments. She seemed quieter. More at ease. Even her breathing slowed down a little.

"Can we get you something, honey?" Mrs. Schnayerson asked nervously. "Anything at all?" She and her husband had been watching nervously from the doorway.

"Sweetie, Miss Pooch is a d-o-g." Mr. Schnayerson spelled the word slowly and carefully. "She can't really understand what you're saying. And even if she could, she can't talk, so what good would it do, anyway?"

"Honey, I was talking to Alicia," Mrs. Schnayerson replied patiently. "Did you really think I was talking to Miss Pooch? That's funny."

"I fail to see the humor in the situation," Mr. Schnayerson replied somewhat defensively.

"Could you bring Miss Pooch some leftovers?" Alicia asked, ignoring her parents' bickering. "She's crazy about chicken teriyaki. Dogs in labor need lots of energy, the pamphlet says." Alicia certainly did seem to know what she was doing.

"And we'll have to make sure you don't get dehydrated. Won't we, Miss Pooch?" Alicia went on as she massaged the bullwawa lightly on her tiny shoulders. "Maybe you could bring in her water bowl, too."

Miss Pooch looked up at her gratefully.

Alicia's take-charge approach seemed to have a wonderful effect on her. In fact, Alicia was coping with the birth of the puppies with unusual skill and grace.

"I hope we're not too late," Mrs. Wiggins said as she rushed into the garage followed by Thomas, Roger, Mr. Wiggins, and of course, McGrowl. "We came just as soon as we heard the news."

"Is everything okay?" Thomas asked Violet.

"I think so," she replied in a hushed voice.

"Oh, Miss Pooch is doing just beautifully," Mrs. Schnayerson said as she hurried in and placed the food and water on the floor beside the dog. "And so is her labor coach." Alicia looked up modestly.

"We brought disinfectant and some towels," Mrs. Wiggins said breathlessly. "I figured they might come in handy." Mrs. Wiggins loved disinfectant and tended to bring it with her wherever she went, whether it was to the birth of puppies, the circus, or a business meeting.

McGrowl watched all the activity. He was excited and worried and scared. Most of all, he felt utterly useless. All he could do was pace up and down the garage nervously. In other words, he was a typical expectant father.

She's gonna be fine, McGrowl, Thomas beamed over to his friend. *I just know it.* McGrowl looked back at Thomas gratefully.

"You're doing a great job," Roger said to Alicia.

"Thanks, Rog," Alicia answered. "I hope you don't mind if I don't get up. I'm needed on the floor."

"That's okay," Roger said, backing away slowly. "Think I'll go in the other room and sit down. Basketball practice. You know." As he limped off he let out a couple of manly groans of pain. "My foot's a little sore. May have torn a ligament. Or something."

PUPPY TALES

If Alicia hadn't been so busy taking care of Miss Pooch she would have realized that (a) Roger hadn't been limping when he walked in, and (b) it wasn't even basketball season.

Roger would never have admitted it, but he was actually feeling a little squeamish. He knew that if he stayed in the room another second his stomach was liable to react the way it did the last time he ate a whole pizza and then rode the Tilt-a-Whirl at the Towering Pines Amusement Center and Water Park, in Cedar Springs.

"Why don't we *all* go wait in the other room?" Mrs. Schnayerson said. "And leave Miss Pooch and Alicia to their own devices. If they need us, I'm sure they'll let us know."

Everyone joined Roger in the kitchen. Thomas and Violet chewed their nails. McGrowl continued pacing. The parents wrung their hands. The clock on the wall ticked loudly. Seconds turned to minutes.

Nobody said a word. Suddenly, the kitchen door flew open. Everyone jumped up as Alicia poked her head in. "Not yet," she said briskly. And then, "More towels, please."

Mrs. Schnayerson handed her a freshly laundered pile, and Alicia disappeared silently into the other room once more. McGrowl continued pacing nervously back and forth, back and forth.

Thomas sent McGrowl an occasional telepathic *don't worry* message, but the only sound in the room was the wind whistling through bare tree branches outside the window. And Mr. Wiggins's fingers drumming aimlessly on the kitchen table. Mrs. Wiggins stared absentmindedly at the cabinets and wondered if Mrs. Schnayerson would mind if she wiped off some fingerprints she noticed on one of them. Before she had a chance to ask, the kettle on the stove suddenly screeched loudly and Roger jumped up and knocked over his chair. It fell to the ground with a loud crash. "Sorry," he muttered.

"Why bother to hide it? We're all nervous wrecks," Mrs. Schnayerson said kindly. She herself had set the teakettle to boiling and promptly forgotten all about it. She poured everyone a steaming cup of rose hip tea, which calmed them all down. Even McGrowl drank some from Miss Pooch's water bowl.

After what seemed like an hour but was really much closer to five minutes, Alicia's footsteps clattered loudly as she raced into the kitchen. She threw open the door. "Number one. It's a girl!" Then she ran back immediately.

Everyone leaped to their feet in excitement.

"Congratulations, McGrowl," Thomas said, smiling. "You're a dad."

Yes, I am, McGrowl thought. He felt so happy he would have handed out cigars if he'd had any.

Thomas reached over and hugged his

friend. "I'm so proud of you, boy." And everyone in the room crowded around the dog and patted him and offered their congratulations.

Then Alicia came rushing in again. "Two more girls. Mother and daughters are doing just fine." Without waiting for a response, she dashed off yet again. This time she didn't return for quite a while.

Finally, Mrs. Schnayerson broke the silence. "I'm going in there. I can't take it any longer." She got up and headed for the garage. She stopped herself, went back into the kitchen, and sat down again. "No, I'm not."

McGrowl paced. His nails clicked smartly on the floor, his collar jangled. And still nobody spoke. Was something the matter? Suddenly, Alicia could be heard shouting from the other room, "It's a boy, it's a boy!" Everyone went running out to see.

CHAPTER EIGHT
The Morning After

The Wigginses and the Schnayersons and McGrowl entered the garage, careful not to make a sound. Miss Pooch lay exhausted but happy right in the middle of her special cushion, surrounded by four tiny balls of wriggling fur. She nudged them gently with her tiny pink nose, urging each puppy closer to her. They needed their mother's warmth to stay healthy and well.

It's amazing, Thomas thought to himself. *No instruction manual. No user's guide. Nothing. She knows just what to do.*

The puppies looked more like rolled-up socks than anything else, but to McGrowl they were the most beautiful things he had ever seen. He practically glowed with pride. Thomas patted him gently. *Good boy*, he thought.

Mrs. Schnayerson mouthed a sincere congratulations to Miss Pooch and Alicia. The poor girl was so tired she could barely keep her head up.

"Proud of ya', Ali," Roger said, hobbling in at last.

Mr. Schnayerson was especially impressed. "Those little puppies are darned cute," he said as he took out his camera. McGrowl walked over carefully and stood proudly beside Miss Pooch and the puppies as Violet's dad snapped the first photo of the happy family.

One of the puppies rolled around on her back and kicked her little legs in the air. Miss

Pooch licked her on the nose. The puppies couldn't bark yet. Instead, they all made soft contented mewing sounds.

Like little kittens, McGrowl beamed to Thomas. And then he caught himself. *Except a million times cuter,* he quickly added. Thomas received the telepathic message and grinned.

"One thing's for sure," Thomas announced to the group. "They don't look like their parents." It was true. None of the puppies looked anything like either a golden retriever or a bullwawa.

"Maybe we should call them golden bullwawatrievers," Violet suggested.

"Try fitting that on a birth certificate," Thomas joked.

Suddenly, the one boy struggled to his feet, and with a little help from his mother managed to stand for a moment or two before falling back onto the pillow. He was a little larger than the rest and obviously a little stronger. "Wait a minute," Thomas said excitedly. "*That one* looks just like McGrowl."

"He's a regular McGrowl junior!" Mrs. Schnayerson exclaimed. "Will you look at that?" On closer inspection the puppy did indeed resemble his father. He had a short, fuzzy blond coat, big floppy ears, McGrowl's prominent brown nose, and large paws at the end of his spindly legs.

"What'll we call him?" Violet asked.

"He's McJunior, of course," Thomas quickly replied. *He certainly is,* McGrowl thought. *Good name.*

Mr. Wiggins spoke at last. "And he couldn't be cuter," he said, sounding relieved that not one of the dogs had attacked him yet.

McGrowl was in total agreement. He went over and ever so carefully nudged his son over to Miss Pooch's side. In a minute all four puppies and their mother were fast asleep, a tumble of multicolored, gently snoring fur.

A band of exhausted Schnayersons said good-bye to an equally tired bunch of Wigginses. Everyone was back in their beds and under their toasty quilts in record time.

"Congratulations, pal," Thomas said as his eyes began to close. McGrowl lay at the foot of the bed and thought about his good fortune. He was a father. He couldn't believe it. He found each of his puppies enchanting. He couldn't wait to teach them everything he knew. And he knew a lot.

He peppered his boy with telepathic questions. *Can we go back in the morning? Can they come and sleep over with us sometimes? What do we name the others? Will they get bigger?* He wasn't the least bit sleepy. He had his very own family.

Thomas fell asleep before he even had a

chance to reply. He dreamed of puppies and snowmen and a Christmas morning that as far as he was concerned had already arrived several days ahead of schedule.

McGrowl was still awake when the sun rose and filled Thomas's room with the bright glow of yet another icy winter morning. He carried over his leash and his snow boots and placed them on the foot of Thomas's bed as noisily as he could. Thomas didn't even stir. And then McGrowl trotted over to the boy and breathed on his face. Thomas awoke with a start.

"Huh? Who? What's going on?" he asked sleepily.

Can we go over now, please? McGrowl begged. *It's really late.*

It was six o'clock in the morning.

Later that morning, when Thomas and McGrowl returned from visiting the puppies, Thomas saw his father in the den. Mr. Wiggins was torturing himself about his life-altering decision. Last night's birth of the puppies had been a compelling diversion, but with the harsh light of day came the harsh light of reality.

Mr. Lundquist, ever the stern boss, had given Mr. Wiggins a deadline. "Decide by New Year's, Wiggins," he had said, "or all bets are off." Mr. Wiggins was busily doing what any sensible person would do. He was making a list of all of the pros and cons and then consulting a Ouija board. So far neither method appeared to be bringing him any closer to a conclusion.

"Congratulations on the birth of y'all's puppies, son," Miltie Gompers said to Thomas and McGrowl as they entered the kitchen. "Ah heah theyah awful nahce." If Miltie did turn out to be Smudge in disguise, Thomas was hardly thrilled to learn of his interest in McGrowl's puppies.

"Thanks, Mr. Gompers," Thomas replied coolly. "I'll send your regards to Miss Pooch."

"Youah nawthern hospitality is puttin' owah southern hospitality to shame, Stacey Wiggins," Miltie said to his cousin, as he dug into his eggs and muffin. "Ya'll's eggs are somethin' spayshel. Yum, yum."

"Thanks, Miltie. Can I make you some more?" Mrs. Wiggins asked politely.

"Well, if y'all gonna twist mah arm lahk thayat, how ken ah refuse?" Gompers said, holding out his plate. Then he announced that he was going to town with Burlington.

There's something wrong with the man's story, Thomas thought. *It doesn't add up. Why did he come to stay with us in the first place? And what is his special bond with my mom?* As far as Thomas could see, his mother didn't appear to like Miltie very much.

Thomas sent McGrowl a telepathic message. *Let's get out of here. We'll hide outside until Gompers leaves and then we'll follow him.*

Good idea, McGrowl replied. *I'd like to find*

out once and for all what he's doing here. With the puppies around, McGrowl knew they needed to be more cautious than ever.

Burlington, who had been upstairs taking a bath in the sink, came screeching down the stairs. "I hate you, *awk*!" she cried.

"We're gonna go to Violet's house again, Mom," Thomas said. "We'll be back in time for dinner. Promise."

"While you're there, why don't you see if the Schnayersons want to bring the puppies over for our tree trimming on Tuesday?" Mrs. Wiggins asked.

"Sure, Mom," Thomas said, and hurried out the back door. He and McGrowl hid behind a holly bush and waited for Gompers and Burlington.

"*Awk*, McGrowl, *awk*!" Burlington shouted the minute she and Miltie left the house. She had spotted the tip of the dog's bushy yellow tail sticking out from behind the bush.

McGrowl quickly withdrew his tail, and he and Thomas followed at a safe distance as Miltie and Burlington made their way along the snowy sidewalks and into the heart of town.

"Think they saw us?" Thomas asked McGrowl.

Count on it was the dog's swift telepathic response.

Gompers went in and out of every store in town. He emerged from a drugstore with a brown paper bag, and he exited Lady Linda's Lovely Emporium with a neatly wrapped snowflake-covered package.

McGrowl pressed his nose up to the window of a pet store when Miltie Gompers went inside and spoke in hushed tones to the shop owner. At one point Burlington shrieked and flew right over to the window where McGrowl had been staring, as if to say, "Look over here, there's someone spying on us." Miltie did indeed look over suspiciously, but by then

McGrowl had managed to hide behind a parked car, and Thomas had turned his back to the store and started walking away in the opposite direction.

"He's onto us," Thomas whispered to McGrowl as they both sprinted around the corner.

McGrowl had to agree. Miltie and his talented parrot were clearly aware they were being followed. They glanced around furtively as they left the pet store with yet another mysterious object hidden carefully away in yet another brown paper bag. *What are these two characters up to?* McGrowl thought as he stared through their packages with his X-ray vision.

All he could make out was a chew toy, some brightly colored lace napkins, and a box of chocolate-flavored liver snaps.

Miltie and Burlington boarded a bus and headed back in the direction of the Wigginses' house. Thomas and McGrowl watched as they chugged off into the distance. They would be safe, at least for the time being. They would continue to monitor the movements of the two visitors carefully.

It was a bright sunny day, but the temperature was well below freezing. As they waited for the next bus back, Thomas pulled his scarf up around his ears and buttoned the top button on McGrowl's red-and-green-checked coat, all the while silently thanking his mother for insisting on winter underwear.

And then the bus finally arrived, and Thomas and McGrowl hopped on board and headed for Violet's house. While McGrowl thought about how much he looked forward to seeing his puppies, Thomas thought about Miltie. Perhaps Miltie Gompers really was precisely who he appeared to be: an unfortunate relative from out of town with bad taste in pets.

PUPPY TALES

Could it be possible? Were the powers of evil actually marooned on a desert island building castles in the sand, instead of here, tormenting Thomas and McGrowl?

McGrowl had to admit he was stymied by the apparent lack of anyone who even slightly resembled Gretchen Bunting. Not even the mistress of ingenious disguises herself could shrink to the size of a parrot and learn how to fly. Where could she be?

Was she waiting in the wings while Smudge prepared the way for her grand entrance? Had McGrowl already encountered her and let her slip right through his paws? With Smudge and Bunting, you never knew what they were up to until it was too late.

CHAPTER NINE
The Name Game

In a few minutes Thomas and McGrowl were warming up in the Schnayersons' cozy kitchen. Thomas sipped hot cocoa from a mug, while McGrowl drank his from a bowl on the floor. *Can I have more marshmallows, please?* he asked Thomas, telepathically.

Thomas scooped up another handful from the bag on the table and dropped them into McGrowl's bowl.

"Forever?" Violet asked, her eyes widening. Thomas had just explained his precarious situation regarding Wauwatosa and the potential family move.

"It's not like it's definite or anything. It's just 'on the burner,'" Thomas said, echoing his father's choice of words.

"Well, I hope someone takes it off of there. And soon," Violet said. McGrowl sent Thomas a telepathic message: *My sentiments, exactly.*

"Wawa — what was that again?" she asked softly.

"Wauwatosa," Thomas repeated.

"Sounds like bad breath or something," Violet joked. "I wouldn't move anywhere with a name like that."

"Never gonna happen," Thomas said.

"Of course not," Violet echoed. But in her heart Violet wasn't really as certain as she seemed. And neither, unfortunately, was Thomas.

"Got any suggestions?" Alicia asked as she

shuffled into the kitchen. She was still in her pajamas, exhausted from her long night of labor coaching. "We're naming the puppies." She carried a big pad of lined yellow paper in her hand.

"Since it's so close to Christmas, have you thought about McClaus?" Violet asked.

"Not really," Alicia replied. "We're thinking more along the lines of, oh, say, 'McDog.'"

"What about McPup?" Thomas suggested. "That's sort of like McDog."

"I love it," Alicia announced, and immediately wrote down the name on her pad.

I do, too, McGrowl thought. *What about McBark?* the dog suggested telepathically.

"How do you feel about McBark?" Thomas volunteered.

"Not bad," Alicia said as she wrote the name down and stared at it. "Looks good in print."

"Do you think that really matters, sweetie?"

Mrs. Schnayerson asked as she walked in and poured herself a cup of coffee.

"How about Rover? Or Spot," Mr. Schnayerson suggested as he wandered in, reading the morning paper. "Those are nice names."

"Daddy, you can't give Miss Pooch's puppies just any old names. They're more special than that," Alicia explained.

"Well, there's Clarence. That's always been a personal favorite of mine," Mr. Schnayerson said as he buttered a piece of toast. McGrowl's head shot up and he gave a bark of alarm. He hated the name Clarence and refused to call one of his children that.

"You've got to be kidding, Daddy," Alicia moaned.

"Honey, who ever heard of a dog named Clarence?" Mrs. Schnayerson laughed. "That's a ridiculous name for a dog. It's a ridiculous name for a person."

"There are millions of dogs named Clarence," Mr. Schnayerson persisted. "They're all over the place."

"Name one," Alicia said.

"Well, I can't actually think of one at the moment. It's been a long night," Mr. Schnayerson explained.

"I thought we already settled on McJunior for the boy," Violet added.

"Good point," Mrs. Schnayerson said diplomatically.

"My mom suggested McGirl," Thomas said, changing the subject.

"I like that," Mrs. Schnayerson commented as she sipped her coffee.

McGrowl barked in agreement.

"I have an idea," Thomas suggested. "Why don't we see which names the puppies like?"

"Great idea," Mr. Schnayerson said, and Thomas and the Schnayersons headed straight for the garage. The puppies were rolling around on the pillow next to Miss Pooch, already playing together. Miss Pooch was trying to get some rest. McGrowl walked over to her and nuzzled her on her spiky little head. She growled affectionately and then dropped right off to sleep.

McGrowl lay down on the floor next to her. One particularly lively puppy tried to pull his big ears with her toothless little mouth.

"That one sure looks like a McBark to me," Alicia said. "Here, McBark," she called. The puppy turned her head in Alicia's direction. "I think she likes her name," Alicia said happily.

"Then McBark it is," Mr. Schnayerson proclaimed. "Here, Clarence," he called. Not one of the dogs budged an inch. "Oh, Clarence," he called, louder this time. "I don't think they hear very well," he said glumly.

"Here, McPup," Mrs. Schnayerson called. The chubbiest little puppy rolled over onto her back and begged to have her stomach tickled. Violet couldn't resist. She kneeled down and patted the tiny puppy ever so gently on her downy stomach. "Guess that one's McPup," Mrs. Schnayerson declared.

"Here, McGirl," Violet called. The last remaining puppy ambled shyly over to her and plopped itself down on Violet's hand. She licked Violet's fingers with her incredibly soft little tongue. "It seems we've named them all," Violet said, smiling.

"That's good, because they're all invited to our house for the tree trimming," Thomas said enthusiastically as he put on his coat and scarf. "And now we'll know what to call them."

McGrowl dragged over a blanket with his teeth and carefully placed it on the sleeping Miss Pooch. He smoothed the edges with his paws until he was satisfied she was well covered. He watched his puppies playing peacefully together and finally left with Thomas.

CHAPTER TEN
Boughs and Bow-wows

By the time Mr. Wiggins came home with the Christmas tree strapped securely to the roof of his car, the Schnayersons had already arrived with their puppies and were comfortably ensconced in the living room. The house was aglow from the lights of twinkling holiday candles, and Mrs. Wiggins was mulling hot apple cider on the kitchen stove.

Thomas and Roger rushed out and helped Mr. Wiggins carry in the fine, tall Douglas fir. Mr. Schnayerson helped Mrs. Wiggins rearrange the living room furniture to make space for the tree. After they had carried it into the house, careful not to scratch the freshly painted walls with its long flowing branches, Thomas and Roger leaned the tree carefully against the living room wall. It instantly filled the house with its fresh, woodsy scent. Mr. Wiggins ran to get the tree stand from its place of honor in the garage.

Miss Pooch yipped happily as she watched her puppies scamper about. McGrowl, for his part, made sure that none of the lively little fur balls got into any trouble. It wasn't easy. McBark was mischievous and loved trying to chew on anything and everything. Her shining dark eyes twinkled as she attacked shoes, lamp cords, and even table legs with her toothless little mouth. McGrowl chased after her, removing everything he could from her path of destruction.

McJunior was a clown. He loved to climb and jump and poke his nose into things. He was always falling off of something. Chairs. Tables. He even fell out of the cardboard box in which Alicia had tried to keep him in. He had precious little control of his spindly legs and large paws and would tip over at the slightest provocation. He didn't seem to mind. He just picked himself up, shook himself off, and started all over again. He seemed to be daring his father to rescue him.

McGirl was gentle and somewhat timid. She did her best to stay out of trouble. McPup was roly-poly and relaxed. She couldn't move very quickly and was easier to keep up with than her siblings. But all in all, keeping up with the four puppies was an exhausting job, even for a dog with bionic powers.

"I love it," Mrs. Wiggins said, admiring the tree. It stood majestically in the center of the living room. "It's even better than last year's!" As Mr. Wiggins and Roger held on to it, Thomas and Mr. Schnayerson tied one end of a rope around its sturdy middle and the other around the window pulls.

Last year's tree had fallen over on New Year's Eve and nearly landed on Mr. Wiggins's Uncle Mort, who had had one too many glasses of eggnog and tried to chin himself on one of the taller branches. This year, no chances would be taken. The new tree was so tall it nearly touched the ceiling.

McGrowl sniffed the tree's freshly cut base eagerly. He found the idea of bringing a tree into the house very intriguing. But then humans never ceased to amaze him. The dog wasn't exactly sure what the tree signified, but he had come to associate its presence in the house as a sure sign that another kind of "presents" would soon be on the way.

McGrowl ran over to the fireplace, poked his large fuzzy head as far into it as he could, wagged his tail expectantly, and waited for Santa to arrive. He listened patiently for the jingle of sleigh bells. Miss Pooch ran over to see what he was doing. McGirl and McJunior came scrambling after them, nipping cheerfully at their parents' heels.

Thomas quickly sent McGrowl a telepathic message: *Not yet, pal.* McGrowl looked back at Thomas sadly. *But soon, boy, I promise,* Thomas said.

"How's your basketball injury doing, Rog?" Alicia asked. She was once again paying her usual amount of attention to Thomas's brother, now that the puppies were born.

"Good as new," Roger answered quickly. Anxious to change the subject, he pointed to McGrowl who was still looking longingly at the chimney. "What's he doing?"

"Looking for Santa, I believe," Mrs. Wiggins said as she emerged from the kitchen carrying a tray of cider and beautifully decorated gingerbread people.

"He doesn't come until later, McGrowl,"

Mrs. Wiggins explained patiently. "He's still up in the North Pole making presents and getting ready for the trip."

"He can't understand a word you're saying, honey," Mr. Wiggins reminded his wife as he warmed his nearly frozen fingers in front of the fireplace. "You do know that."

"Sometimes I wonder," Mrs. Wiggins replied as she put down the tray and picked up a few stray pine needles that had fallen onto the carpet. McGrowl came over to her and nuzzled her leg. It was the closest he was able to come to telling her she was right — that he did, in fact, understand every word she said.

Then he padded quickly into the dining room to rescue McJunior, who had gotten into trouble again. The adventurous little puppy had managed to climb up one of the dining room chairs and had nearly made it onto the table. McGrowl stopped him just in time, held him firmly but gently in his mouth, and put him back on the floor. Then McGrowl ran into the den to stop McBark from eating the fringe off Mrs. Wiggins's favorite throw pillows.

Mrs. Wiggins carried out several boxes of tiny lights, and everyone helped string them around the tree. The puppies were so happy they could barely contain their excitement. All four of them danced around under the lower branches and swatted at the lights with their front paws. Poor McPup was so pudgy she fell over every time she tried to jump.

"We should have named her McChubby," Roger said, laughing.

"Shh, Rog," Alicia warned. She put finger to her lips. "She'll hear you. We don't want to make her feel self-conscious."

"Sorry, McPup," Roger said guiltily. "I just meant you were really cute."

When the lights were hung, Thomas and Violet brought up from the basement a number of carefully labeled cardboard boxes

containing the Wigginses' Christmas ornaments. The ornaments had been collected
over many Christmases past. Some of Great-
gramma Gompers's handblown glass ornaments were put away there. She had brought
them over from Europe ages ago when she
was still a child.

Thomas turned the radio to station WCDR,
which was playing twenty-four hours of
Christmas music, and everyone listened to
"Deck the Halls" while they actually did deck
the halls. Or at least the hallways. Mrs.
Wiggins had brought out yards and yards of
pine boughs, and both families wound them
in and around the banisters and the mantel-
piece and the window ledges.

Then it was time to decorate the tree. Soon
its boughs were sagging under the weight of
every type of glass, wood, and china ornament. Thomas's favorites were festive globes
of colorfully decorated paper and cardboard.

They had been made during World War II,
when glass and metal supplies were scarce
and everyone had to make do with whatever
was on hand.

"Do you think he's going to — you know?"
Mr. Wiggins asked nervously as McGrowl cir-
cled the beautifully trimmed tree several
times, as if preparing to give the tree his ulti-
mate seal of approval.

"Of course not, dear," Mrs. Wiggins replied.

She had spoken too soon. McGrowl was so
exhausted from running after the puppies all
evening, he saw the tree and forgot he was
inside. Without even thinking, he lifted up one
hind leg as he prepared to give the tree his
own personal holiday greeting.

"Watch it!" Mr. Wiggins yelled.

*Santa is watching, pal. We're talking major
reduction of gifts. We're talking coal in your
stocking.* Thomas had accompanied his father's cry with his own telepathic warnings.

The dog instantly got the message and quickly lowered his leg.

Just kidding, McGrowl beamed back to Thomas sheepishly.

"Great cookies, Mom!" Roger exclaimed as he attacked the platter of gingerbread people. He always ate the arms and legs first and saved the heads for last.

"Thanks, but your Dad made them," Mrs. Wiggins explained as she took out a bag of popcorn garlands and handed them out. "I didn't have time."

"Well done, Pop." Thomas smiled as he polished off a gingerbread dog in the shape of McGrowl. "Didn't know you were such a good cook."

Can I have one? McGrowl asked. *I promise I'll be good.*

"Can McGrowl have one?" Thomas asked.

"Of course," Mrs. Wiggins replied, and

handed the dog his very own Miss Pooch cookie. McGrowl took it carefully between his lips and brought it over to the puppies, who begged eagerly for a bite. He broke the cookie into equal bite-size chunks and fed a piece to each one of his children. The puppies yipped and pushed and jumped, eager to get a bite of the sugary snack. McGrowl didn't spill a crumb. He was eager to get back in Mr. Wiggins's good graces. Thomas's warning had made a big impression on him.

"Look how careful he's being, honey," Mrs. Wiggins said, nudging her husband. "He's a wonderful father. And so are you, honey," she added, giving Mr. Wiggins an affectionate pat on the cheek.

Mr. Wiggins had really outdone himself. He had thoughtfully re-created the entire Wiggins and Schnayerson households out of gingerbread. Even Miltie Gompers was represented by a particularly rotund sprinkle-laden cookie. A tiny sugar parrot sat on his shoulder, frowning miserably.

"Say, where *is* our favorite guest?" Thomas joked as he bit off a piece of Miltie's head.

"He rushed out to do his last-minute shopping," Mrs. Wiggins said, sipping some cider. "He'll be back any minute."

He sure does a lot of shopping, Thomas thought.

"Who wants to help put on the tree topper?" Mr. Wiggins asked as he removed a delicate china-and–papier-mâché angel from its well-worn box. McGrowl barked an affirmative *woof*. He came trotting over and picked it up gently in his teeth.

McGrowl padded over to the ladder and started climbing up slowly, paw after paw, until he reached the top and placed the glittery creation on top of the tree. "Well done, boy," Thomas said, and went over to plug in the lights. The tree shimmered and twinkled magically. Everybody stood back to admire it.

"Remember, honey?" Mr. Wiggins asked Mrs. Wiggins. "I gave you that angel for our first Christmas."

"How could I ever forget?" Mrs. Wiggins smiled. "It was my only present from you, and I loved it so."

"And we sang Christmas carols, and my mother came over, and you burned the turkey."

"And we had hot dogs for dinner." Mrs. Wiggins chuckled. "And we had a wonderful time."

"I loved that Christmas."

McBark barked happily. It wasn't a loud bark. But it was a bark. McJunior tried to climb up the tree, and nearly broke an ornament. Miss Pooch gave him a warning growl, and he stopped right away.

McGrowl came running over to Mr. and Mrs. Wiggins with a sprig of mistletoe in his mouth.

He stood on his hind legs and tried to hold it up over Mr. and Mrs. Wiggins's heads. He couldn't exactly reach, but Mr. Wiggins gave Mrs. Wiggins a kiss anyway. Thomas and Roger looked at each other and rolled their eyes.

And then the doorbell rang, and Miltie came rushing in, parrot on shoulder. "Sorry ah'm late. Did ah miss the whole thang?" he drawled.

"I'm afraid you did, Miltie," Mrs. Wiggins said. "But there are still some cookies left."

"*Awk*. Birdy wants a cookie, *awk*," the parrot screamed, and made a dive for the platter. McGrowl stood firmly in front of it, growling protectively. He had had just about enough of that annoying bird. McGrowl sent Thomas a message: *If she takes one bite, she's toast.*

Burlington seemed to get the message. She flew away and perched on a branch of the tree. "Touchy, touchy. *Awk*," she complained as she glared down at McGrowl.

And then Thomas noticed that Miltie wasn't carrying a single package. Whatever he had been doing, it wasn't shopping. McGrowl noticed as well.

Miltie began to sing the verse to "Winter Wonderland" in a curiously mellifluous voice. "Over the hill lies a mantle of white . . . " By the time he had reached the chorus, both families joined in using their loudest and most joyous voices. "Sleigh bells ring, are ya listnin'?" could be heard several blocks away at Mabel Rabkin's house. The elderly registrar looked up from her table, where she was enjoying a wonderful meal with her grandson, and smiled sweetly at the sounds.

McGrowl joined in with his best bass howl, and Miss Pooch gave a few high-pitched yips. She wasn't as musical as McGrowl, but she had a lot of spirit. And then all the puppies gathered around and howled along with their parents.

McJunior threw his little head back and howled the loudest of all the puppies. He howled so loudly he knocked himself over and tumbled into McPup, who rolled over and landed on McGirl and McBark, who fell over, too.

McGrowl and Miss Pooch nudged the puppies back up on their feet, and everyone went right on howling as if nothing had happened. Thomas looked at McGrowl's new family and sighed. *How can we leave all this?* he thought. *This can't be our last Christmas in Cedar Springs. It just can't.*

CHAPTER ELEVEN
Bad News

The next few days went by in a blur of shopping and wrapping and puppy-sitting. And then, on Christmas Eve, everyone at the Wiggins and Schnayerson households hung their stockings on their chimneys with care and went to bed dreaming of Christmas morning. The puppies each had their own tiny stockings that Alicia and Violet had knitted just for them.

McGrowl stayed up half the night listening for sleigh bells with his bionic hearing and then fell asleep shortly before Santa made his arrival. He must have, anyway, because when McGrowl awoke and sneaked downstairs the next morning, the stockings were filled to overflowing with candy and surprises, and beautifully wrapped presents were piled high beneath the tree.

McGrowl bounded back upstairs to wake up Thomas and Roger. But suddenly, the phone rang loudly and woke up everybody before McGrowl had a chance to do the job himself.

An exhausted Mrs. Wiggins rubbed the sleep from her eyes, grabbed blindly for the receiver, and then dropped it twice before she managed to successfully hold it to her ear. Mr. Wiggins snorted and spluttered and put on his glasses.

"Are you absolutely certain?" Mrs. Wiggins asked after a moment. "When did you find out? Uh-huh. I see. That's terrible. We'll be right over." She set down the receiver, wide awake. She got dressed and ran to the boys' room to tell Thomas and McGrowl and Roger the bad news.

"I'm sure everything will be perfectly fine, but —" she said as she searched for just the right words to convey the problem. "There seems to be an issue with one of the puppies." She paused again. "McJunior."

"What is it, Mom?" Thomas asked, trying not to panic. McGrowl cocked his head to one side and nervously waited for more information.

"He's probably perfectly fine, but . . ."

"What is it? What happened?" Roger demanded. "Is Alicia okay?"

"She's fine. Everyone is probably fine. It's just —" There was simply nothing to do but come out with it. "He's missing."

"Missing!" Thomas exclaimed.

Missing! McGrowl thought.

"Who's missing?" Mr. Wiggins asked.

"McJunior," Mrs. Wiggins said, "He seems to have wandered off. Nobody panic." But before she could stop him, McGrowl was racing down the stairs with Thomas at his heels. He ran to the front door, waited for Thomas to open it, and was outside and galloping down the driveway before Mrs. Wiggins even noticed what was happening. He didn't even stop to put on his booties. The remaining Wiggenses grabbed scarves and sweaters and jackets as they ran to catch up.

Miltie and Burlington strolled into the kitchen just in time to peek out the window and see four anxious people and a dog racing down the icy street, throwing on their hats and mittens as they ran. Miltie casually made a pot of tea and gave Burlington a cracker.

"I hate crackers, *awk!*" the obstinate parrot squawked before she gobbled up the tasty treat. Then Miltie took a long hard look around the house, ran to the closet, pulled out his notepad, and started to put his plan into action.

The Wigginses and the Schnayersons stood in the garage and shook their heads in disbelief. McGrowl started searching the room for clues. Miss Pooch was curled up on the floor, trembling. She was surrounded by McPup, McGirl, and McBark — but McJunior was nowhere to be seen. The puppy had disappeared. McGrowl started searching the room for clues.

"Think, Miss Pooch, think," Alicia said, between sobs. "Where did McJunior go? Try to remember." All Miss Pooch could do was look around nervously and whine. McPup and McGirl realized something terrible was happening and clung to their mother anxiously. Even the brave McBark looked miserable as she comforted herself at her mother's side.

McGrowl's quick search determined that

McJunior was, indeed, missing and not simply hiding under a box or a blanket as
McGrowl had hoped. *Hopefully he hasn't
gone very far,* McGrowl thought. He was less
than one week old. It was fifteen degrees outside. How far could he have gotten?

Try to remain calm, he told himself.

While the Schnayersons and the Wigginses
were combing the backyard looking for
footprints, McGrowl noticed something.
Something that sent a chill running down the
back of his powerful neck. In all the excitement, he had failed to notice a small opening
near the rear of the garage. It wasn't very big.
At first glance it appeared as if some boards
had simply rotted away, leaving a gap between
the floor and the wall. Closer inspection
revealed that someone had pulled away the
boards from the support beams. A very strong
someone.

Pieces of wood were lying inside the

opening, and some of the boards were bent and cracked. Unless you looked very closely you would never have even noticed the damage. And then McGrowl saw that if you pushed at the wall in just the right place, it swung back and forth like an old gate.

Someone had carefully created an undetectable entrance. Large enough for that someone to gain access to the garage without going through the house. And small enough for no one to notice. McGrowl had a feeling he knew just who that someone was. He sent an urgent telepathic message to Thomas.

"You guys look around the house," Thomas said, receiving the message and pulling up his hood. "McGrowl and I are gonna search the neighborhood."

"I'm coming with you," Violet said.

"I'll stay here," Alicia said. "I need to watch over Miss Pooch and the other puppies."

"I'll look upstairs," Mrs. Schnayerson

suggested. "Maybe he's gotten into the laundry. He likes laundry." Mr. and Mrs. Wiggins agreed to accompany her.

"I'll go ask the neighbors if they noticed anything unusual," Mr. Schnayerson said. "Roger, why don't you come with me?" he suggested. And everyone rushed off to search.

McGrowl tried to find tracks, but the newly fallen snow had covered up what clues there might have been.

"Come on, McGrowl," Thomas pleaded. "Can you find his scent?"

To McGrowl, each of his puppies had a decidedly different odor. Like a fingerprint, no two were exactly alike. McJunior's particular scent reminded McGrowl of warm woolen mittens. He did detect a bit of it on a branch near the driveway. He sniffed eagerly, following his nose across the street and down the alley between Doris Mueller's house and the Appletons' garage. Thomas and Violet followed fast on his heels.

"What's the matter, kids?" Officer Nelson asked as he watched them poking around in some trash cans in Mr. McSorley's driveway.

"One of McGrowl's pups is missing," Thomas said urgently. "We've looked everywhere."

"Gosh, that's terrible," Officer Nelson sympathized. "I'll put out an APB." He pulled out his walkie-talkie, dropped it in the snow, searched for it, found it, and wiped it off. "Missing puppy. Repeat. Missing puppy!" he shouted into the machine.

McGrowl picked up McJunior's scent again and started running in the opposite direction. The dog zigzagged this way and that. He followed McJunior's trail up driveways, and around mailboxes, and into the street. The puppy seemed to have taken a path that made absolutely no sense at all.

"Can you describe the missing animal?"

Officer Nelson asked Thomas, taking out his notepad and jogging along beside him and Violet.

"He looks exactly like McGrowl," Thomas responded. "But a lot smaller."

"Curly blond hair. Big nose. Large paws!" Officer Nelson hollered into his walkie-talkie as he struggled to keep up.

Meanwhile, McGrowl sped down the street. He looked into every house with his X-ray vision. Perhaps the freezing puppy had been taken in by a kindly stranger and was simply waiting to be discovered. On the other hand — and it was looking more and more likely — the dog could easily have been kidnapped. Was Smudge up to his usual tricks? Was he using McGrowl's only son as bait to lure McGrowl into a devilish trap? McGrowl hated to admit it, but it was all beginning to make sense.

He thought of Miltie and Burlington and all of their suspicious behavior. The constant shopping. The way they never came to the Schnayersons' with them. It all added up.

McGrowl sprang into action and turned to face Thomas. He had a brilliant idea. *We've gotta get the lie detector. We're gonna talk to Miltie. It's our only hope. Quick.*

Thomas listened intently to the telepathic message. Of course. The lie detector. At last they'd have a chance to put their device to use.

"What's he telling you?" Violet asked.

"No time to explain," Thomas explained. And the dog and the two children were off like a shot.

CHAPTER TWELVE
Homeward Bound

And so, while the Wigginses and the Schnayersons searched vainly in and around Violet's house, Thomas and Violet and McGrowl made a quick trip to the basement, unnoticed, and raced back, lie detector in hand, to Thomas's house.

In the meantime, Thomas did explain to Violet how Smudge-as-Miltie probably stole the puppy, and how the lie detector could prove his guilt.

They got there just in time to see Miltie and Burlington leaving quietly through the back door. McGrowl cornered them both. He barked ferociously. They backed away in fear. They were trapped.

"Don't shoot, *awk*!" the parrot screamed.

"What is goin' on heah?" Miltie demanded.

"We think you're up to no good," Thomas said boldly, clutching the lie detector.

"We think you stole McGrowl's puppy," Violet added.

"Theyah's been a mistake," Miltie said, cowering. "Ah haven't done anythin'. Me and mah bird are perfectly innocent. Ah can explain everythin'."

In less time than you could say "Milton Smudge and Gretchen Bunting," Miltie was sitting at the kitchen table, hooked up to the lie detector and answering Thomas's questions.

"What planet are you from?" Thomas demanded. Thomas had to ask a certain number of obvious questions in order to establish what was known as a baseline reading.

"Earth, ah believe," Miltie answered. "Is that some kahnd of trick question?" Dozens of wires led from his arms and legs over to a scary-looking black box on the floor. He wore a large metal helmet on his head, on top of which sat a frightened-looking Burlington. The parrot, for once in her life, remained strangely quiet.

Thomas studied the man's response. So far, at least, he appeared to be telling the truth.

"What did you do this morning?" Thomas asked.

"Nothin' much," Miltie began, smiling weakly. "This and that."

"Get to the point, please," Thomas said as he fiddled with the dials. "We don't have much time."

The detector's dials whirred and whizzed and recorded every one of Miltie's bodily responses. But it didn't take a machine to observe the beads of sweat pouring off Miltie's forehead, his nervously twitching hands, and the shifty look in his beady little eyes.

"Ah didn't do anythin' this mawnin'. Ah was jus' goin' out for a walk in the fresh ayah. That's all."

"I don't believe you," Thomas said boldly. "You're lying."

One glance at the monitor had revealed that Miltie's numbers were off the chart. His heart rate had nearly doubled, his skin temperature had risen dramatically, and his pulse had shot up very high. He had clearly been caught in a lie. There was no doubt about it whatsoever. The machine was an unqualified success. Now, all they had to do was find out what Miltie and his bird had done with the puppy.

"What's going on?" Violet whispered.

"We're about to find out," Thomas said quietly as he adjusted the knobs on the lie detector and asked the most important question. "What did you do with McJunior? The truth."

Before Miltie had a chance to respond, McGrowl growled menacingly. Tears welled up in Miltie's eyes.

"Your dog is frightnin' me. Could you tell him to back off?"

"Not until you tell us the truth, Milton Smudge. What did you do with that puppy?" Thomas demanded harshly.

"What puppy? I don't know anything 'bout a missin' puppy," Miltie pleaded. "And why are you calling me 'Smudge'?"

Violet tugged at Thomas's sleeve insistently. "Could we talk?" she whispered.

Thomas looked at his friend curiously. Why was she getting in the way of the investigation? "What's up?" Thomas whispered back.

"Something's fishy," she began. "If he really was Milton Smudge he'd have tried to escape by now or to trap us in some way."

"You may have a point," Thomas admitted. "I'm going to ask him another question."

"Okay," Violet replied. She and McGrowl stared closely at the machine as Thomas questioned the man again.

"Tell us everything you did this morning," Thomas ordered, trying to sound as official as he could. He had never interrogated anyone before in his entire life.

Miltie began. "It's a secret. Ah don' wanna tell y'all."

McGrowl walked over to the man and stared right into his face. And then he bared his teeth and snarled. Violet jumped back, startled. She had never heard McGrowl make such a frightening sound. Even McGrowl was taken aback.

"Aw right," Miltie said, through clenched teeth. "Ah'll talk."

"I want to know everything," Thomas said. "Start at the beginning."

"Ah was born in 1952 in a little shack out-sahd of Cleveland, Ohio. It rained that day. Mah mothah's name was Blanche."

"Not *that* beginning. What did you do this morning?" Thomas interrupted. He was in no mood to play games.

Thomas sat back and watched the dials as Miltie told his story. Every word of it was one hundred percent true. The dials and needles of the lie detector confirmed everything.

"Ah got up. Ah had some breakfast."

"Go on," Thomas urged.

"And then ah got out the presents."

"What presents?" Violet asked. She knew Thomas was supposed to be doing the inquiry, but she couldn't help herself.

"Mah Christmas presents."

"Why would you take out Christmas presents?" Thomas asked, still staring at the machine. So far, what Miltie was saying was the truth, the whole truth, and nothing but the truth.

"Becawse it's Christmas, and in mah family we put out the presents thayan."

"But why were you sneaking out of the house just now?" Thomas asked less harshly.

"Ah ran out of wrappin' papah, and I was goin' out to get some moah. That's all," Miltie confessed.

In all the excitement everyone had forgotten that it was, indeed, Christmas. McGrowl looked at Miltie curiously. Had he possibly misjudged the man?

"Really?" Thomas asked, wide-eyed.

"Yes, really," Miltie answered. He was beginning to lose his patience. "Why would ah lie about a thang like that?"

"Let me ask you point-blank," Thomas continued. He was beginning to think that he had made a terrible mistake. "Did you have anything to do with the kidnapping of Miss Pooch's puppy?"

"No!" Miltie replied emphatically.

"Are you sure?" Thomas asked.

"Of cahwse ah'm shuah. Why would ah steal a puppy? Ah already have a pet." Burlington shrieked proudly in agreement.

"Well, then, I've made a terrible mistake and I'm really sorry," Thomas said as he flushed with embarrassment and rushed to detach Miltie from the lie detector.

"We knew you were telling the truth all along," Violet lied. "We were just being extra careful."

"Right," Thomas added quickly. "We hope you're not upset."

"Ah thank I can forgive you," Miltie said at last. "It is Christmas, after all."

McGrowl scratched his big furry head with his paw, confused. If Miltie Gompers wasn't

Milton Smudge, then where was McJunior, and what in the world was going on?

Suddenly, there was a loud crash in the living room, and Thomas and McGrowl and Violet raced in to see what was happening, while Miltie and Burlington recovered in the kitchen. There, on the floor right where he had landed, was McGrowl's missing puppy.

Looking dazed and confused and a bit embarrassed, the little dog tried to shake the debris off his coat and promptly fell over. He was so little he could barely stand up. But he had found his way to his father. That morning he had missed him, and he had gone out looking for him before everybody had gotten up, and he became lost. When he detected McGrowl's scent at the Wigginses' house, he had simply walked through the wall and into the house to get to his father.

It was obvious to everyone. McJunior had,

of course, inherited each and every one of McGrowl's superpowers. It was he who had chewed on the walls of the garage until he had weakened them. It was McJunior who had managed to push on the boards and make an opening for himself.

He had also broken a puppy-size hole in Mrs. Wiggins's wall and tracked mud and ice and melting snow all over her brand-new carpet.

Milton Smudge had not returned to kidnap the puppy after all. McGrowl breathed such an enormous sigh of relief he blew the puppy off his feet. McJunior got up, shook himself off, and walked shakily over to the Christmas tree. He lifted up his hind leg and prepared to welcome it in his own special way, just as he had seen his father do.

DON'T DO IT! McGrowl thought. And lo and behold, the little dog looked over at his father and cocked his tiny head intently, as if he were carefully listening, which indeed he was. He got up immediately and trundled obediently back to McGrowl. *Good boy,* McGrowl thought as he put a powerful front leg around the little dog and hugged him gently.

Daddy, I'm hungry. The puppy had sent his father a telepathic message. He looked up at McGrowl with his big brown eyes and whimpered softly. Thomas heard the request as well and ran into the kitchen to get a bowl of milk. Violet ran back home to tell the others that the puppy was safe and sound. McGrowl looked up at the Christmas tree. The angel at the very top seemed to be winking down at him.

"Merry Christmas, McGrowl," it seemed to be saying. "I hope you enjoyed your gift."

CHAPTER THIRTEEN
Well Done

The lights on the tree twinkled brightly. The turkey sat in the middle of the table, browned to perfection, surrounded by mounds of mashed potatoes, and cranberry sauce, and walnut apple stuffing. Santa and his elves and eight plastic reindeer danced across the mantel. It was the perfect setting for the perfect Christmas Day meal.

The Schnayersons, the Wiggenses, and Miltie Gompers and Burlington all sat together in the Wigginses' dining room. Mr.

Wiggins had put an extra leaf into the table earlier that day.

Everyone had a napkin neatly tucked in their lap or under their chin. Or below their beak. Or beneath their muzzle.

McGrowl and Miss Pooch sat proudly under the table, and all four puppies lay next to them in the big carrying basket. Mr. Schnayerson had decorated it with ribbons and bows and brightly colored stars and a cheery red-and-green-plaid blanket.

McBark, McPup, and McGirl lay on their sides, sleeping soundly, exhausted from the adventures of the day. Miss Pooch had already fed them their Christmas dinner before coming over. Only McJunior was awake. He jumped around eagerly, trying to get out of the basket, as usual. He finally managed to work himself over to the edge and fell with a gentle *splat* on the rug. McGrowl picked him up gently in his mouth and carefully deposited him back in the basket with his sisters and issued a simple telepathic command. *STAY.*

McGrowl knew he would have to keep a special eye on McJunior. No one was to know that he had inherited his father's special gifts. And with those gifts came added responsibility. He would grow up and help McGrowl in his fight against evil in the unlikely event Smudge and Bunting ever returned.

"I'd like to propose a toast," Mr. Wiggins began. "Let us raise our glasses high. To dear friends and neighbors. To long-lost relatives and their parrots. To dogs and puppies everywhere — but especially under this table."

Then Mr. Wiggins cleared his throat and looked very somber. He spoke again: "I've made a very serious decision. My family and I will be moving to the lovely village of Wauwatosa, Wisconsin, soon."

Thomas groaned when he heard the name of the dreaded place. With all the excitement of the puppies and Christmas, he had nearly managed to forget about the possibility of moving. Violet shot Thomas a look that seemed to say, "How could you do this to me?" McGrowl peered up and gave Thomas a similar look. Having just found his lost puppy, he was about to lose him again. He moaned a low, sad moan of regret. Alicia and Roger exchanged mournful looks. Even Burlington looked miserable. "Phooey! *Awk!*" she cried. "Phooey!"

Only Mrs. Wiggins had been informed of the life-altering decision in advance. Not that it made her feel any better. Mr. Wiggins had made up his mind while he was stuffing the turkey. He just couldn't pass up the great new opportunities the job offered him. He had confided in Mrs. Wiggins while she was basting the very same bird some moments later.

Mrs. Wiggins had become so disturbed she nearly dropped the entire platter of food on the floor.

"It's going to be fine," he continued. "We'll still visit Cedar Springs. There will be many letters." But he was almost drowned out by McGrowl's soft wails and Alicia's accompanying sniffles.

Milton Gompers got up from the table abruptly and holding his notepad, went over to Mr. and Mrs. Wiggins and whispered in their ears. "Excuse us for a moment, if you will," Mr. Wiggins said as he and Mrs. Wiggins and Miltie and Burlington scurried into the den to have a private discussion.

A hush fell over the table. Even Miss Pooch was quiet. She seemed to know that something important was being decided. The distant voices of some carolers wafted into the room. "Frosty the Snowman was a jolly, happy soul. . . ." Thomas was so anxious he could hardly sit still.

Meanwhile, in the den, as Miltie Gompers told his incredible tale, Mr. and Mrs. Wiggins sat on the sofa, listening.

"Ah owe everythin' ta y'all, cousin Stacey, and ah thank it's hah tahm y'all heard the story," Miltie began. "It all started about fawty yeahs ago when ah was a little boy, and y'all were a little girl. Y'all were so kahnd ta me. Ah could nevah forgetcha." Miltie asked Mrs. Wiggins if she remembered something important she had done for him.

"It was somethin' *quite* impo'tant," Miltie prodded. "Thank hard, now." Stacey Wiggins thought and thought but she couldn't remember. So Miltie reminded her. When Miltie was ten, Stacy had loaned him some money. "A bully had come along and stolen my whole lahf savin's. I was cryin' and cryin'. We didn't have much money to begin with. I jus' didn't know what to do."

And then Mrs. Wiggins's memories came rushing back to her. Miltie was a sad little boy. His knees were always skinned, and his face was always dirty. He didn't seem to be able to stay out of fights. She could still see his tearstained face as he ran up the driveway. He was screaming after Billy Colletti, the bully who had stolen his money, "Come back, come back!"

Stacey didn't even think twice. She ran to her piggy bank and removed its entire contents. All thirty-seven hard-earned dollars. She put the money in a paper bag, and she brought it to Miltie and gave it to him. Just like that.

She'd said she didn't need it. She'd said she had found most of it on the street, anyway. "And when you find somebody else's money," Stacey had said to Mealy Miltie, as he was commonly known, "you basically have to give it away. It's bad luck if you don't. Everybody knows that."

Mr. Wiggins was amazed to hear the story. "You never told me," he exclaimed, looking at his wife in awe.

"I'm ashamed to say I had forgotten all about it," Stacey explained. "Until this very minute."

"Well, ah didn't," Miltie continued. "It meant so much ta me. Ah knew that story about fahndin' the money and it bein' bad luck an' all wasn't really true. But ah believed it anyways. And it gave me mah dignity back. Ah owe everythin' . . . everythin' to you."

Miltie went on to explain that he became interested in the stock market at an early age and invested the thirty-seven dollars that Mrs. Wiggins had given him in a computer company. The stock grew and grew. By the time Miltie eventually sold the stock, the thirty-seven dollars had grown into a fortune, enabling him to create a successful though little-known Internet business called whereareyou.com. Miltie had devised an ingenious method of locating long-lost relatives through arrangements with federal and national agencies throughout the country. Which happened to be precisely the means by which he had discovered Stacey Wiggins's current address.

Along the way, Mealy Miltie had managed to pay off each and every one of his family's creditors and clear the family name. It seems that Miltie wasn't really so mealy anymore.

"Ya'll didn't just help me, Stacey," Miltie explained. "Y'all helped mah whole family."

"What a beautiful and fascinating story," Mr. Wiggins said. He couldn't help wondering where it was leading.

"Y'all won't believe what ah just came up with," Miltie said, getting to his point. "The idea hit me like a pie in the face. It jus' came raht at me," he explained.

"Ah am gonna' invest heavily in the Momsicle business. That is, if y'all will let me," he said, and then went on to explain that Momsicles were a real winner, but as he put it so bluntly, "The business plan stinks."

"How so?" Mrs. Wiggins asked. Miltie explained the dangers of undercapitalizing in a growth-dominated market and the importance of a national release pattern, including local television saturation. Mrs. Wiggins invited her cousin to join the company on the spot.

Miltie was thrilled. Burlington suddenly shrieked, "Hallelujah!" It was the first nice thing anybody had ever heard her say.

Miltie laid out his plan. In exchange for fifty-one percent of the common stock, he would invest half of his sizable liquid assets in Momsicles, Inc. With the sudden influx of cash, Momsicles could afford the publicity needed to go national. Mr. Wiggins would run the marketing division. The company would carefully build regional sales, eventually culminating in an Initial Public Offering that would net the Wigginses more money than they had ever dreamed of.

Best of all, as the newly appointed head of national sales and promotion for the entire Momsicle account, Mr. Wiggins did not need to take the job in Wauwatosa and could remain in a town he could spell, and that he and his family loved.

"The two of y'all git along so beautifully ya' maht as well be wukkin' together," Miltie said as he put his arms around Mr. and Mrs. Wiggins. "Do we have a deal, y'all?"

Mrs. Wiggins nodded her head and joyously exclaimed, "We shuh do have a deal, y'all," in her very best southern accent.

Mr. and Mrs. Wiggins and Miltie raced back into the room. Burlington swooped up to the top of the tree and sat right next to the angel. "Announcement, *awk!*" she shouted. "Announcement!"

"Stop the presses, folks," Mr. Wiggins said. Thomas's heart was pounding. McGrowl sat up as straight as a statue and his ears perked up. He didn't want to miss a word of what was being said.

Mr. Wiggins proceeded to relate the entire saga of Miltie and his money and his wonderful decision to invest in the Momsicle business. Everyone in the room listened, rapt, to the entire story.

When Mr. Wiggins got to the part about staying in Cedar Springs and not having to move to Wauwatosa, Wisconsin, (which Violet had taken to calling Halitosis, Wisconsin), everyone at the table stood up and cheered. McGrowl barked so loudly he woke up the puppies, who joined in the uproar.

Every single one of Thomas's wishes had

come true. Nobody seemed to notice when he crawled under the table and gave McGrowl and Miss Pooch and the puppies his own special Christmas wishes. The wishes included hugs and pats and all the cookies Thomas had been able to hide in his pockets.

When the last candle had burned itself out and everyone had eaten every last bite of food, opened up every last present, and gone home or upstairs, Thomas and McGrowl went to bed.

"What a day!" Thomas said to McGrowl. "What a night!"

The boy and his dog looked out their bedroom window. Thomas had on his new pajamas with the cowboys on them, and McGrowl had on his new collar and tags. A full moon cast its gentle glow across the snowy mounds that covered Thomas's front lawn.

Thomas couldn't believe his good fortune. They were staying here. He got under the covers and pulled his pillow up around his ears. McGrowl got up on the bed, next to him. Thoughts of puppies danced through the head of boy and dog alike. *Better than sugarplums,* Thomas thought. McGrowl couldn't have agreed more. They would spend tomorrow with the puppies, and the day after as well. Milton Smudge and Bunting appeared to have truly disappeared. Thomas was looking forward to handing in his science project after the vacation. He was feeling pretty confident. It had survived its field trial beautifully.

McGrowl snuggled tightly up against Thomas's side. *For once,* he thought, *I can go to sleep without worrying about a single thing. My boy is well and my puppies are safe. What a wonderful feeling.*

CHAPTER FOURTEEN
Fast Forward

Winter came and went, and now it was spring. Thomas had grown nearly an inch since Christmas, and Violet had become a full-fledged member of the Girl Scouts of America. Mr. Wiggins grew an inch, too. In the waist. Just as Miltie (who had departed soon after Christmas) had predicted, Momsicles were thriving. And so were McGrowl's puppies. McGirl and McPup weighed nearly fifteen pounds. McBark was even bigger. The three girls had grown into perfect combinations of their mother and their father. And just as Violet had said, everyone referred to them as "golden bullwawatrievers."

McJunior was the largest of all of them. With his sleek golden coat, his big soulful brown eyes, and his large tan nose, he reminded Thomas a lot of the McGrowl he had first encountered that rainy afternoon in the woods nearly two years ago.

On one warm spring day, Thomas and Violet ran around Thomas's lawn, playing Frisbee with the puppies. "Watch those flowers, McBark!" Thomas called. "Good catch, McGirl!" he shouted.

"Jump a little higher, McPup," Violet encouraged.

McJunior sat by Thomas's side waiting patiently for his turn. McGrowl ran around showing his puppies proper form and catching an occasional Frisbee himself. Miss Pooch watched proudly from the sidelines. She loved seeing McGrowl with his offspring. He was a kind and patient father. And all of the puppies loved spending time with him.

Just then Thomas caught sight of something out of the corner of his eye. A flash of gray tail was all he needed to see to know that Olivia the cat had stopped by to torment McGrowl. McGrowl, of course, had noticed as well. He sent Thomas a message. *Not even interested,* he reported.

I'm proud of you, boy, Thomas replied.

Someone else *was* interested, however. McJunior went hurtling down the driveway before McGrowl could issue a single warning. McGrowl followed his son in a blur of yellow fur. Although Thomas ran after them, chasing a bionic dog and his bionic puppy made about as much sense as chasing the wind.

Soon Olivia had shimmied up the tall elm tree that conveniently grew in front of her owner's house. Out of harm's way, she stared down at McJunior from the tallest branch and taunted him mercilessly. *"Hsssss!"* She arched her back. McJunior was not about to take this kind of behavior lying down. He started climbing the tree as easily as if it were a ladder. The cat hissed even louder and started running for another branch. McJunior was getting closer. The poor cat was cornered.

Just then McGrowl arrived. *Get down from there immediately or no dessert, ever,* he ordered his son.

No fair, Daddy. She started it! McJunior complained to his father.

It doesn't matter, McGrowl said in his sternest telepathic voice. He had to try hard to keep a straight face. He knew exactly how McJunior felt. He often felt the same way himself.

McJunior climbed down from the tree immediately. The puppy loved food as much as his father did. *Good boy,* McGrowl thought, and he and McJunior trotted back toward the Wigginses' house. The cat looked down, relieved. She would annoy McJunior another day.

McGrowl rejoined the puppies, Miss Pooch, and Violet on Thomas's lawn. Soon the happy bunch was playing Frisbee again, yipping and barking. In a little while it would be summer vacation, and McGrowl would teach his puppies how to swim and play in the sand, and how to chase a beach ball. And a wave.

Thomas would go to sleepaway camp, and Violet would, too. Eventually, Thomas knew, they would watch McGrowl's puppies grow up into big dogs, with families of their own. And their puppies would call McGrowl McGramps.

Thomas could hardly wait.

Bob Balaban is a respected producer, director, writer, and actor. He produced and costarred in Robert Altman's Oscar®- and Golden Globe–winning film *Gosford Park,* which was named Best British Film of 2001 at the British Academy Awards. He appeared in *Close Encounters of the Third Kind*, *Absence of Malice*, *Deconstructing Harry*, *Waiting for Guffman*, *Ghost World*, *The Mexican*, and *A Mighty Wind*, among many other films, and appeared on *Seinfeld* several times as the head of NBC. Bob produced and directed the feature films *Parents* and *The Last Good Time*, which won best film and best director awards at the Hamptons International Film Festival. Bob lives in New York with his wife, writer Lynn Grossman, and his daughters, Hazel and Mariah. At the moment, he is canine-less, but he is looking forward to a close encounter with his own actual dog, not just one of the literary kind.